Attack
of the
Spider
Bots

ZONDERKIDZ

Attack of the Spider Bots
Copyright © 2009 by Robert West
Illustrations © 2008 by C.B. Canger

Requests for information should be addressed to:
Zonderkidz, *Grand Rapids, Michigan 49530*

Library of Congress Cataloging-in-Publication Data

West, Robert.
     Attack of the spider bots / by Robert West.
        p.   cm. – (Star-fighters of Murphy Street; bk.2)
     ISBN 978-0-310-71426-2 (softcover)
     [1. Christian life – Fiction. 2. Science fiction] I. Title.
PZ7.W51933At 2008
[Fic]–dc22
                                             2008007361

Published in association with the literary agency of WordServe Literary Group, Ltd., 10152 S. Knoll Circle, Highlands Ranch, CO 80130.

Zonderkidz is a trademark of Zondervan.

Editor: Barbara Scott
Art direction & cover design: Merit Kathan
Interior design: Carlos Eluterio Estrada

Printed in the United States of America

Attack
of the
Spider
Bots

Robert West

ZONDERVAN.com/
AUTHORTRACKER
follow your favorite authors

For Bill Myers, gifted writer and filmmaker, unselfish mentor and, best of all, friend.

-RW

Table of Contents

1

The Cave of the Beast

Becoming a teenager is like living in a sci-fi movie. You keep morphing into somebody else while emergencies are popping up all around you.

Case in point: Beamer tripped on the rock steps leading into their secret cave network. As Ghoulie figured out later, it was because Beamer's leg had morphed one-eighth inch longer than it had been the last time he climbed those steps. Then while Beamer was rubbing his scraped knee, Scilla picked up a faint noise. They listened until they heard a distant rumble and a repeating clank.

They called themselves Star-Fighters—Beamer, the exile from California; Ghoulie, the African-American

brain trust; and Scilla, the girl who could do anything a boy could, only better. They got the name because of the spaceship they found high up in Beamer's tree. It didn't seem like much at first. After all, it was only a ramshackle wooden tree house shaped like a spaceship—no graphics card, no 3-D accelerator, nothing you could shove into an Xbox. But, hey! You know what they say about looks being deceiving. That broken-down plywood box had already taken them to places no kid has gone before. And, in the process, they were finding a lot of strange worlds right where they lived—that being an ancient, pothole-ridden lane, only one block long, named Murphy Street. This cave labyrinth was one of those weird worlds.

Up till now, though, they'd used the caves mostly as just a shortcut home from school. But an unexplained clank, Beamer thought, was a good reason to start some big-time exploring. After all, a rumble could be lots of things—an earthquake, rushing water, whatever. A clank, though, was something else. Nothing in nature clanked.

So they were off. Beamer and Ghoulie were following Scilla, who was holding a lamp to light the way. She tracked the clanking and rumbling sounds up, around, and through the winding, cobweb-infested network of caves beneath Murphy Street. Luckily there weren't that many bugs, rats, and mice in winter. As usual, Scilla led them to a dead end.

"Scillaaaaa!" Beamer complained, remembering the time Scilla had led them into a brick wall when they were being chased by Jared and his bully goons. Now they were facing an unmovable rock wall. Actually, it was a pretty interesting wall. Symbols and pictures had been scratched or painted all over it—Native American, he guessed.

"Hey, it's not my fault!" Scilla protested. Putting her ear to the wall, she listened. "Don't you hear it? The clanking sounds are coming from the other side of the wall!"

After putting their ears to the wall, Beamer and Ghoulie had to agree that Scilla was right. "Okay, Plan B," Ghoulie said. "The Indiana Jones maneuver." As if the wall was one big pinball machine, they started punching and pulling every symbol and protruding rock they saw, looking for a trigger that would open a hidden door.

Finally, when their fingers were seriously throbbing, they stopped. "There's got to be another way in there," Beamer said, blowing on his finger. "Let's backtrack."

That's what they did until they found a side tunnel. Careful to scratch little rocket symbols into the wall so that they could find their way back, they again struck off into the unknown. Making one turn after another, trying to head in the direction of the clanking sound, they fought through major spider colonies and piles of rubble. Suddenly they heard another sound, this one loud and shrill. Scilla stopped abruptly and shouted, "Go back!" But it was too late. The next thing they knew there was a one-eyed creature with bad breath wailing like a banshee hot on their behinds. That's *hot* as in "burn-your-buns hot" and getting hotter by the second. The Star-Fighters ran down a dark tunnel as fast as their middle-school legs could go, which wasn't all that fast since they had to run bending over like orangutans. The trouble was that the tunnel was so small they couldn't stand up—not even Scilla. Frankly their prospects didn't look good. In fact, you might want to see if anything is written on the rest of the pages. This could turn out to be a very short story.

Just an hour before, on their way home from school, the threesome had decided to take their subterranean shortcut. It wasn't all that short when you considered that they had to take a long ladder beneath the park, wind through a maze of caves, and then come back up and cut through a bizarre garden behind Parker's Castle. That "Castle" was Murphy Street's own little corner of Transylvania—dark towers, moat, and all. It belonged to Ms. Parker, who just happened to be the scariest person on the street.

Shortcut or not, that passage beneath Murphy Street had saved their hides more than once. It was their emergency escape route and their hideaway from bullying gangs. This summer, the caves had been lit up like Christmas from the clouds of fireflies and the moss glowing on the walls. With the coming of winter, though, the fireflies were burrowing into their tiny winter caves, leaving only the dim, creepy glow of the moss for illumination. That might be enough if you're a bat, but not if you're human.

Luckily the lanterns still worked, if you could really call them lanterns. After all, lanterns were supposed to have a flame, right? These didn't; instead, when you turned one on, it had a large round bulb filled with glowing liquid. The eerie part, though, was that the light was the same color as a firefly's light. Of course, the really eerie part was that no one knew who made them or how they worked. But somebody had made enough of them to place all over the caves so that you could find one when you needed it.

That was a good thing, since you couldn't always count on having a flashlight when an emergency turned up—like the one they were having now.

The bad news was that a lantern had guided them into the tunnel they were now wishing they could find a way out of. The good news? ... They were still young, and their parents could probably get discounts on their tombstones.

The beast was almost on them, with its hot, steamy breath making them feel like shrimp on a barbie. Suddenly the tunnel floor slipped out from beneath them.

"Aiiiiiiiiii!" they cried as they flailed momentarily in midair. Then they fell. The next thing they knew, they were plunging through a chute—as in a water ride—and splashing into a fast-moving stream. The sound echoed all around them. They had the sense of being in a large space.

"Help, help!" Ghoulie burbled as he splashed the water frantically. "I can't swim!" Then he saw Scilla standing up, hands on hips, looking down at him with a smirk. He felt his knees bump against the streambed and stood, giving Scilla a sheepish, red-faced look.

"What was that thing?" Beamer sputtered as he crawled, drenched and muttering, out of the stream.

"I don't know," said Scilla, "but it could use some work on personal hygiene. I can still smell its breath."

"Next question," Ghoulie said as he peered through the darkness. "Where are we?"

A faint light grew in the distance ... behind a range of hills.

"Are we outside?" asked Scilla. "It can't be night already."

"Worse than that. It looks like sunrise," groaned Beamer. "It's almost time for school."

A soft line of light slowly crawled across the landscape, revealing more hills and valleys, then roads and a village. There was a church with a steeple, a train station, shops—some with windmills—and a group of houses.

"One thing's for sure," said Scilla. "We're not in Middleton anymore."

Something didn't seem right about the scenery. Beamer couldn't quite put his finger on it. Again they heard the beast scream, and they whirled around to see the one-eyed monster charge across a double-arched bridge.

"It's ... it's a train!" cried Ghoulie.

Now there was enough light to see that the eye was the headlamp for a steam locomotive. *Looks about the size of our living room sofa*, thought Beamer. That was when he realized what was wrong—the scenery was miniaturized!

"Holy tamole! D'y'all mean we're trapped in somebody's train set?" asked Scilla.

2

Lost World

"Well, for what it's worth, it's not your everyday train set," said Ghoulie as he tripped over a water mill. "Ouch! There aren't many train sets you can stroll through like a walk in a park."

"It's a whole other world," said Beamer, "built inside a cavern!"

Beneath the bridge was a miniature mountain stream into which they had fallen. Farther away was a waterfall, which cascaded down a cliff to feed the stream. Somewhere back there was probably a wall, but the painting was so real that it looked like the range of mountains stretched for miles. The sky, too, seemed infinitely high above them, with wisps of clouds moving across—*Moving*! *The clouds were moving*! Beamer thought with a start. He couldn't even see the projectors. The illusion was so incredible, it made him dizzy just thinking about it. *Maybe they weren't in a cavern after all!*

"Hey, do you suppose we've been transported to some faraway place inhabited by tiny people?" asked Beamer. "I could get used to a Gulliver lifestyle."

"Yes, but that's a very tiny sunrise for a real world," said Ghoulie, pointing to the brightening horizon.

Beamer took a couple of steps over the rail yard and the train station. There was a fair amount of animation. Cars, trucks, and vans—old ones—moved along the streets and highways. How old? Well, definitely way before Beamer's time.

"They couldn't be real, could they?" Scilla asked as she kneeled down to look at a garden of miniature flowers.

"Oh, sure," answered Ghoulie. "Lots of plants can be grown in miniature—azaleas, cyclamen, and rhodo-something. Um," he added as he stretched to see past a miniature hill. "I think I see an entire pumpkin patch beyond that ridge."

At that moment, Beamer heard the whine of propeller-driven airplanes. He spun around to see a miniature squadron of WWII fighter planes diving toward him.

"Hey! We come in peace," he announced like he'd dropped in from Neptune for a chat with the president. The whine of the planes grew louder. "Now hold on there," he gasped as he started to back up, "I'm just a kid. Only really bad guys kill women and children." Suddenly their guns fired. He started to dive to the ground, but not before he felt pings all over his body. "Ow! Ouch! Cut that out!" he cried as he swiped at the little pellets. "I'm being strafed!" Before he knew it Beamer was giggling and jerking about, laughing out of control. All those tiny pellets were driving him crazy! "Stop ... Stop it!" he cried frantically between bursts of laughter.

Finally, the planes whisked past him and disappeared. Breathing heavily, Beamer's giggling turned into a gasp.

"Whoa! Tickle warfare," he wheezed, "the world's next weapon of mass destruction."

Scilla was still laughing—at him. "You were so funny," she guffawed. "You were jerkier than the scarecrow in *Wizard of Oz*."

"Right—a barrel of laughs." *She'll get hers*, he vowed. Finally breathing easier, Beamer looked up. He didn't think the ceiling was high enough for clouds to form naturally, but sure enough, one particularly dark cloud that was too low to be a projection was moving closer.

Seeing the cloud's shadow on the ground, Scilla looked up just in time to get dowsed by a shower. She squealed in a pitch high enough to break every chandelier in Parker's Castle.

"Serves you right! Don't melt!" Beamer yelled, feeling a sweet sense of revenge.

Scilla muttered angrily as she wrung out her shirt sleeves. "Go ahead and laugh, y'all. I wanna find the joker who's runnin' this thing!" she spit out. "I don't like his sense of humor."

"What if nobody's running it?" asked Ghoulie with a shrug.

"D'ya mean it could be totally automated?" asked Beamer. "That's ridiculous! Somebody's got to take care of all this." He looked around the cavern. "Come to think of it, somebody's gotta let us out of here!"

"I wouldn't count on a visit anytime soon," answered Ghoulie. "I don't know if you guys noticed while you were doing your comedy routine, but this little world has a fairly high arachnoid population."

Spiders! Beamer didn't see any of the creepy little things, but there were plenty of cobwebs, and they weren't miniaturized.

"The animation keeps some places clear," said Ghoulie, as he leaned down and ran his finger across the dome of an observatory. "But that's too deep a buildup of dust for a housekeeper to ignore," he added, showing Beamer a glob of dust thick enough to be icing on a cake.

Scilla waved her lantern to wipe away a cloud of spider silk. Beneath it she saw a house that looked like a miniature of Parker's Castle. "Hey, y'all!" she cried as she leaned down to look in a window. "Look what we've got here."

"What?" asked Beamer as he made his way over to her. Ghoulie was right beside him, and they dived in for a view at the same time.

"Hey!" she cried as she slipped down to her knees. "There's a train set in this little house that looks like a miniature of the one we're standing on!"

"Does that train set also have a miniature Parker's Castle?" Beamer asked, shaking his head.

"This is getting too weird," said Ghoulie with a sigh. "And don't even think of asking if our Parker's Castle and Murphy Street are in some giant train set."

"Hmmm." Beamer scrunched his face thoughtfully as Ghoulie continued.

"Anyway, it's a good bet that we are under Parker's Castle."

"But when you think of it," said Scilla, "Old Lady Parker doesn't seem the type to play with train sets."

"Yeah, you've got that right," grunted Beamer. "So who's the engineer?"

Suddenly a loud blast and a *woosh* brought them leaping to their feet. A small rocket on a fiery tail was climbing up in front of a city skyline. It arched across the sky and disappeared. A moment later they all took a deep breath.

"Is that city supposed to be Middleton?" Scilla asked, turning her head sideways for another look."

"Looks more like the Emerald City to me," said Beamer as he climbed over a range of hills. True enough, in contrast to the quaint village near the stream, the city was ultramodern, with highways winding in and around the city like silver ribbons. "Here's the space port!" exclaimed Beamer. Yep, there were spaceships—old-style ones with fins—sitting on their tails on little launchpads. As he watched, one pad rose from below, carrying another ship to replace the one that had just taken off.

Beamer suddenly noticed that the artificial sun had moved all the way across the artificial sky. It was beginning to turn dark. "Hey, we gotta get out of here," he barked. "Who knows what happens in this place after dark."

"But how?" asked Ghoulie.

"Uh, what's wrong with the way we came in?" Scilla asked before Beamer and Ghoulie could work themselves into a panic.

"Trouble is," said Ghoulie, the middle school brain trust. "I don't think there's room for both us and the train in the tunnel at the same time. We need to clock the train's circuit to see if there's enough time for us to scramble back up into the tunnel and down to our entry point before it comes around again."

Ghoulie pulled back his jacket sleeve to activate the stopwatch on his oversized wristwatch, which included a GPS and an LCD display, as well as Internet access. Yep, if there was a gadget out there, Ghoulie had it.

"Good grief," said Beamer, rolling his eyes. "Take a seat, Scilla. If he's in NASA mode, we may be waiting here till next Tuesday."

"Better safe than sorry, you know," Ghoulie chortled.

While Beamer and Scilla sat morosely on a miniature stone wall, waiting for Ghoulie to time the train's route, their mini-world transformed into night. Shadows grew longer as the soft line of light faded into the horizon. Then the moon rose, not full, just a thin crescent. Beamer wondered if it changed phases like the real moon. A night sky materialized. He could make out the Big Dipper and the constellation Orion. The planets were there too, though not to scale. They were, in fact, much larger than they looked in the real night sky.

"Hey, look there!" shouted Beamer. "You can see the dead volcanoes and canals on Mars." Jupiter had its red spot and Saturn, its rings. A comet, complete with its tail, also moved across the night sky. You could even see one galaxy looking like a whirlpool of light. Somebody had gone all out in the imagination and technology department to create this world.

Scilla had crossed over to look in the window of a tiny flower shop, when a noise brought her to wide-eyed attention. She looked behind her and fell back into the stream. She screamed as she first swam, then crawled, and then ran away from the noise. With her head turned backward, she didn't even notice Beamer until she plowed into him.

Beamer fell *splat* and yelled, "What's the matter? Can't you watch where you're going?" She was already back on her feet and burning shoe leather. "Hey!" he yelled after her. "A little 'excuse me' would be nice." Then he heard an ear-crushing *roar* and whipped around. His face suddenly froze.

3

Escape from Netherworld

Beamer had forgotten how to breathe, let alone move. The beast's huge moonlit shadow was already on him. Finally Beamer's legs began scooting him backward as a gigantic creature covered in scales climbed out of a deep gorge. Somewhere in the back of Beamer's mind was the thought that the beast was probably just another animated toy, but—even in a diminutive state for this miniature world—Godzilla was pretty colossal.

Beamer stumbled and then ran, with the monster's feet thundering behind him. "Forget the timing!" he yelled to Ghoulie. "We've gotta take our chances." Behind him, the beast was squashing cars and buildings and making the world quake. Whether the creature was real or not, they were here without permission, and who knew if somebody hadn't invented this "dragon" to guard its treasure world.

"I'm with you!" Scilla shouted as she splashed through the stream and scrambled up the ravine to the tunnel.

Ghoulie didn't need any convincing either when he saw the towering beast pounding toward him.

Just as Scilla reached the tunnel, the train whistle blew her eardrums into "mute." She jumped back just as the train sped out of the tunnel and roared across the bridge. By the time it passed, Beamer and Ghoulie had caught up with her. Godzilla roared again, and they leaped into the tunnel with a chorus of screams.

Once more they made like hunchbacks running through the tunnel. Afraid that any moment they'd see the "eye" of the locomotive coming toward them, they finally resorted to running on all fours. They made it back to their tunnel exit just as they heard the locomotive screech around the bend.

With enough relief that their legs wobbled, they retraced their way through the caves, following the rocket-shaped symbols they'd scratched into the rock walls at each turn. At one point, they again heard the *clank* that had drawn their attention in the first place.

"Did you guys hear any clanking at the train set?" Beamer asked.

"Not even a *clink*," Ghoulie answered, shaking his head.

"Me neither, now that you mention it," said Scilla.

They gave each other long looks and then glanced once more toward the sound. "Come on," Beamer said as he lurched back toward their familiar exit. "One mystery at a time."

Following their usual route home, they climbed the rock steps out of the caves and cut through a greenhouse filled with glowing plants and birds and into Ms. Parker's strange garden. It didn't look so weird now, covered with snow. There was no sign of its usual population of carnivorous plants, crawling vines, and giant flowers. Finally, they escaped through the side gate which, though no longer broken, was now always left unlocked.

*   *   *   *   *

Snow was one of the few things about this world called Middleton that Beamer liked better than his old home. It never snowed in L.A. Oh, you could see it in the distance, but you had to drive up to the mountains to touch it. Living with snow day after day was something else. Here you could step out your door and play in it all kinds of ways. He couldn't understand why adults complained so much about it. So they had to do a little shoveling along the sidewalk and driveway now and then. But for kids, snow was great. If it snowed hard or long enough, you'd even get out of school once in a while.

Unfortunately, the snow wasn't going to tell Beamer anything about the person who had built that incredible train set. This was too big of a mystery to ignore. A few questions to the neighbors got Beamer started. Mrs. Ringwald, the red-headed woman who wore glasses the size of a small bicycle, had a reputation for keeping up on all the neighborhood gossip. She told him that Ms. Parker had a strange brother named Solomon. Beamer wasn't sure what she meant by "strange," except that she rolled her eyes when she said his name.

Beamer's next step was to check him out on the Internet. The Middleton newspaper's online archives recorded that a "Solomon Parker" had opened a trolley company long before Beamer's parents were born.

Beamer found a picture of a trolley on the Internet. It looked pretty much like a bus. But then he noticed that it had poles on top leading to a grid of wires strung above the street. *So it ran on electricity*, thought Beamer. *But what happened if the driver turned left when the wires went right?* That was when he noticed that trolley wheels looked something like train wheels. Then he realized that a trolley could only go where the tracks let it go, like a train. Beamer took this to be a pretty good sign that Solomon Parker had something to do with the train set.

The big question, then, was why Mr. Parker had left the train set running but abandoned all these years. That proved harder to answer than Beamer expected. For one thing, neither Mrs. Ringwald nor Mr. Springer, who'd been Ms. Parker's gardener for years, knew where Mr. Parker lived. For another, his phone number was unlisted, and his official mailing addresses included the trolley station and a post office box. At least that is what Ghoulie had discovered. All three were in Beamer's bedroom, putting their heads together to find the mysterious Solomon Parker.

"A ghost would be easier to find!" Beamer exclaimed in frustration. "Which, for that matter, is what he might have become by now," he added with a shrug.

"Nope, there's no death certificate, and somebody still picks up mail from that post office box," said Scilla, feeling proud of her detective work over the past couple days.

"Maybe he just wanted peace and quiet and moved to Fiji," suggested Ghoulie as he tapped keys on Beamer's computer.

"Too many tourists," muttered Beamer. "And a really deserted island wouldn't have any electricity. I've got a feeling this guy likes gadgets too much to give up electricity."

"What about askin' Old Lady Parker?" asked Scilla, who had lain back across Beamer's bed. "She's gotta know. She's his sister, after all."

"Yeah, I thought about that," said Beamer with a sigh. "But both Mrs. Ringwald and Mr. Schlesinger—you know, the guy with the long mustache and bushy hair—said they had a big fallin' out years ago."

"But they must have sent each other Christmas cards or birthday cards?" she argued.

"Nope," said Beamer, "haven't spoken to each other for fifty years."

"Wow, that's some fallin' out," said Scilla. "What do you suppose it was all about?"

"Mr. Schlesinger said it was over money, and Mrs. Ringwald said it was over a house," said Beamer. "So who knows? I can tell you one thing: I'm not about to ask Ms. Parker."

"Good thinkin'," said Scilla, sitting up with a gulp. "She's scary enough when she's in a good mood. Who knows what she'd be like if we riled her about the brother she hates."

"So, you're thinking she was in a 'good mood' when we talked to her those months ago?" asked Ghoulie. "If I remember correctly, she didn't smile once the whole time."

"Probably no room left on her face for more wrinkles," quipped Beamer. "Well, at least we've got an address for the trolley station," he said as he leaned over Ghoulie and tapped the Print key on his computer. "Let's see what we can find there."

* * * * *

A teachers' conference gave the kids a day off from school. Beamer, Ghoulie, and Scilla took the opportunity to ride a bus downtown to the address of the old trolley station. The bus crossed a street that still had trolley tracks sunken into the pavement. It was a bit bumpy, but not as much as it would have been if the tracks were totally above ground like train tracks.

When they stepped off the bus, the Star-Fighters stared in shock—except for Beamer, that is, who was immediately smacked in the face by a wind-tossed newspaper. The page wrapped itself around his face like it was going to suck out his brain. When Beamer finally wrestled it away, he too saw the trolley station. It was totally in ruins—fit only for things that crawled or hid in ghostly shadows. In fact, the entire neighborhood was a ramshackle collection of abandoned warehouses—a great place for a mob hit or a CIA rendezvous.

Beamer now realized why the bus driver had raised one eyebrow so high when he showed him the address. The station took up an entire block and was surrounded by a chain-link fence with lots of Keep Out signs.

"Now whadda we do?" grunted Scilla as she plopped down on a bench that was peeled nearly clean of paint. "I don't think we're gonna get much information from the rat population."

"And I think this has to be the coldest spot in the city," muttered Ghoulie, pulling his overcoat tighter around him.

Yeah, as in North Pole cold, thought Beamer. Not that Santa Claus would be found dead here. Frankly it looked like nobody wanted to be here.

"What does it matter anyway?" asked Ghoulie. "Solomon Parker is old news. From the looks of this place, he was history fifty years ago."

"I don't know," Beamer murmured as he sat on the bench and put his elbows dejectedly on his knees. "Something just seems missing. It's like a story with no ending." Beamer suddenly felt a slight tug at his pocket. "Hey!" he yelled as he twisted around. A hand recoiled back through the slats in the bench—a hand holding his wallet! "What are you doing? Stop!" he cried as a boy wearing a hat with earflaps streaked away along the fence.

4

The Forgotten Ice Palace

"Stop, you little thief!" Beamer yelled as he ran. Ghoulie and Scilla, right behind him, also filled the ghostly neighborhood with shouts. Suddenly, the boy ducked down and disappeared. A moment later, the Star-Fighters arrived at the spot and saw a break in the fence. Forgetting all the Keep Out signs, they slid beneath the wire mesh and quickly picked up the chase.

They raced into the broken-down lobby of the trolley station and skated around the tattered benches and shattered ticket windows, taking a few pratfalls in the process. Everything was covered in snow drifts and draped with icicles and frozen cobwebs. The old walls probably hadn't felt the echoes of so much noise for decades. Beamer finally skidded around a corner and out a side door. He slid almost immediately to a halt in the yard. Half a second later, Ghoulie and Scilla crashed into him from behind. Their eyes scanned the area like sonar. The pickpocket had disappeared. His trail of footsteps ended abruptly in the snow right in front of them.

"What did he do, beam up to his spaceship?" asked Beamer in exasperation. He spun around to check out the station's roof. The boy wasn't there either, although he might have found a place to hide up there. It was a complicated roof. There were many roof lines, all steep and crossing each other like a series of mountain peaks. From this angle, seeing it wrapped in drifts of snow, the trolley station didn't look so bad. It had the look of a rambling ice palace.

"Holy tamole! Would you look at that?" Scilla said, shattering Beamer's thoughts.

He followed her gaze. The yard in front of them was a field of rusted-out trolley cars. Though enfolded in waves of snow like a choppy sea, they still stood in perfect order as if waiting to be called back into service.

"Well, I've gotta find my wallet," grumbled Beamer. "It's got my lunch pass and library card. Mrs. Hotchkiss will never believe I lost it like this. That kid's gotta be around here someplace. Let's start checking the cars."

Searching Beamer's room for a lost item was usually about as easy as searching the Amazon jungle, but this was much worse. Most of the trolley doors hadn't been opened since the dark ages before television and were rusted closed. Some were blocked behind snow mounds the size of Mount McKinley. Others were guarded by some impressive ice-coated spiderwebs. Sometimes all they could do was jump up and glance through the windows. A few pogo sticks would have come in handy, especially since Ghoulie hadn't gotten round to inventing anti-gravity boots yet. Beamer's head was beginning to ache from all the jumping, when they finally found what they were looking for.

The snow had been swept away from the rear door of one of the trolleys. And the windows were frosted, which meant that it was warmer inside than out. The door squeaked as they pushed the handle but folded open easily. The inside was free of snow, clean, and almost warm. There were no trolley seats in this car except for the benches that ran next to the wall. There was a lot of clutter, though—pretty much like any boy's room on the planet.

"What is this, his loot?" asked Ghoulie.

"What else? He's a thief, isn't he?" said Beamer. Several stacks of magazines, books, and newspapers were piled up like the Leaning Tower of Pisa (nope, not pizza). *Well, at least the jerk would be able to read the warrant for his arrest,* thought Beamer.

A pile of hubcaps—all polished up—scattered noisily onto the floor when Beamer brushed by them. There were bottles full of coins, an assortment of men's ties, a box of watches, a pile of cigars, and another box full of women's scarves, purses, and shoes.

"Not much of a haul, if you ask me," said Scilla as she picked up a little statuette of the Empire State Building. It was missing its top spire.

"Yeah, I think my mom can do better in a morning of shopping garage sales," said Beamer with a wry grin. He tipped the airplanes and spaceships that were hanging from a rack to make them swing back and forth. Action figures, trucks, and tanks—all missing pieces here and there—were arranged for battle on a bench below.

They moved on toward the back of the trolley and found a few blankets and a ratty pillow set up on a bench next to a heater. "Well, at least it's not too cold here," said Ghoulie. "It looks like he's using propane gas."

"Probably stolen, like everything else," grumbled Beamer.

"Maybe not," Ghoulie corrected as he shook a propane bottle taken from a pile of them. "These are all only part full—probably leftovers that people had thrown away. The trouble is, it can be dangerous to use this stuff inside."

Shirts, pants, and other clothes were hung or draped on window hooks. In the very back of the trolley was a small, beat-up camping stove and some boxes and cans of food. A nearly empty bowl of cereal buried in half-frozen milk was sitting on a small bench.

"All the comforts of home," said Beamer with a smirk. Beamer was angry enough to think about taking the kid's stuff as payback, but then returning thievery for thievery didn't sound quite right. He was pretty sure Jesus wouldn't do it. He'd been taught to ask himself what Jesus would do whenever he wasn't sure about the right choice. Of course, that meant he had to get to know Jesus pretty well. Luckily, although Jesus lived an incredible 2,000 years ago—back in the days of gladiators and emperors—four guys wrote whole books telling his story. No, Jesus wouldn't take something that belonged to someone else, and he wouldn't hurt someone in anger.

"Well, at least we know where the kid lives," said Ghoulie. "We'd better get home. The snow's getting thicker in the sky out there."

Just then they heard a loud *smack* and saw an explosion of white on the front window.

"What was that?" yelped Ghoulie.

"A snowball the size of a cantaloupe!" shouted Beamer as he ran out the door. "Show your face, you thieving wimp!" So much for Beamer's conquest of anger.

"Any sign of him?" asked Ghoulie as he and Scilla came up beside Beamer.

"Nope, but I'm not giving up on this guy. I'll be back!" Beamer shouted like some half-pint Terminator. His voice echoed through the empty lot, but he heard no answer.

The three friends took a few wrong turns, trying to find their way back to the torn patch of fencing. By then, the whirling snowflakes were as thick as chicken dumplings. Beamer still managed to find his wallet, minus a few dollars, lying next to the torn fence. So much for his snow-shoveling money.

"Look at it this way," said Scilla. "The kid didn't have to return your wallet."

Beamer grumbled and muttered to himself as he put the wallet back into his pocket. He gazed one more time at the snow-frosted trolley station as the bus pulled up at the stop.

* * * * *

Later that evening, Beamer told his parents about the boy in the trolley car. The funny thing was they spent more time scolding Beamer for going there than they did knocking the kid for stealing Beamer's wallet. Of course, Beamer didn't know he was going to Middleton's skid row. Their response was that he should have left as soon as he realized it. But then, if he had, they wouldn't have known about the kid living in a trolley car in the middle of winter. *Sometimes parents made no sense at all.*

The next thing Beamer knew, his mother was all over the Internet and on the phone trying to find out what to do about that kid—to find out who he was and how to help him. All Beamer could do was roll his eyes. *Yep, his mom never did anything halfway.*

The next day, Beamer was in his attic getting things to take over to the tree ship. The attic was a pretty good shortcut to the tree, actually. Beamer could climb out the attic window, skitter across the roof a few steps, and launch onto a tree branch for a quick climb over to the tree ship.

The problem was that, to get to the attic window, he had to get past ... the web. Beamer and his family had found the giant web in their attic when they moved in. It was so huge, stretching from the floor all the way up to the apex of the roof, that Beamer's dad had called in some scientists to investigate it. The attic still looked like the engineering deck of the starship Enterprise, alive with blips and beeps, bubbling chemicals, flashing lights, and twisting, illuminated lines from all the electronic and chemical equipment scientists were using to study the now-famous MacIntyre Web. Nobody'd ever seen the mutant octopod that had supposedly built this two-story silk metropolis. Beamer had named it with the scariest sounding name he could think of at the time—Molgotha.

Actually, some of the scientists didn't think the web had been built by a real spider. They thought some person had put it together as a hobby or a joke or a scientific experiment. The trouble with that theory was that the web was made of genuine spider material—DNA positive.

On the other hand, the web did some things that most spiderwebs didn't. Beamer had told the scientists that the web seemed to suck up energy. He'd told them that he had caught a glimpse of it through the attic window, glowing hot the moment before the tree ship had warped into one of their adventures. Unfortunately, nobody past puberty believed that their experiences really happened. Well, at least Beamer always got a good laugh. Sometimes he thought he was cut out to be a stand-up comic, except that nothing else he ever said drew any laughs.

Getting past the web, though, was no laughing matter. Beamer eyed suspiciously the dark corners of the attic, looking for signs of movement or a large flying thread of spider silk. Let's face it, Molgotha—or whoever built that thing—was one top-gun silk architect. He/she/it or his/her/its descendants weren't going to leave it abandoned forever. Beamer sucked in his breath and scooted slowly beneath the sticky little arch the web made above the floor. All Beamer could do, then, was to hope and pray that a gust of wind wouldn't make the web billow, or that he wouldn't accidentally take a breath.

Having already completed that process, Beamer popped his head out the attic window. In the fall, Beamer had wondered if the tree that held the tree ship would lose leaves like the other trees. After all, this tree had its own ecosystem, its own weather pattern, its own insect population, and its own energy field. There could be a windstorm in the tree while the rest of Murphy Street was as quiet as a tomb. As it turned out, the tree did lose its leaves. It seems that the cycle of life rules, no matter what.

Trees always seemed so pitiful when they lost their leaves. They went out in a blaze of glory, Beamer had to admit, with all the red, yellow, and purple colors of fall, but then they were left looking like skeletons of their former selves.

When snow came, though, the picture was totally different. Those naked tree limbs were coated a glistening white with icicles draped all over them. The whole treescape shimmered and twinkled like a magical fairy land—if you believed in such things.

It was a little tougher working on the tree ship when you

were wrapped up like an Eskimo, but Beamer's mom always insisted he dress warmly. Ghoulie and Scilla got the same lecture from his nanny and her grandmother. Actually, it turned out to be a good thing, because whenever any of them rocked the tree, they'd suddenly be pelted by a load of snow bombs from the branches above.

At the moment, the tree ship had its own layer of snow frosting with icicles hanging all over it like Christmas decorations. "How's it going up there?" he yelled at Ghoulie through the attic window.

Ghoulie winced as an icicle drop fell into his eye. He wiped it off and went back to tucking wires into the instrument panel. "How should I know?" he shouted back irritably. He was supposed to be making a universal translator, but that wasn't easy to do when you didn't have all that good a grip on your own language.

Beamer snickered to himself. Nobody could juggle numbers and electrons around better than Ghoulie, but, at the moment, he wasn't on the best of terms with verbs and adjectives. Oh, he could talk circles around anyone and used words big enough to strangle a normal person's brain, but diagramming sentences in English class drove him nuts.

"D' ya'll need any help?" yelled Scilla as she swung up onto the trunk where it crossed into her yard.

"No, I think I've almost got it," Ghoulie shouted. "Okay … it's finished … I think," Ghoulie said with a shrug. "At least it's as finished as I can make it." All he'd done was load word processing and voice recognition software into the ship's computer and attach a microphone and a speaker. Just reading English was going to be a stretch. "Universal" it was not. All

Ghoulie could hope for was that when they and the ship warped into one of their adventures, it would work just as well as everything else did. Let's face it: in the real world, a plywood ship in a tree had little chance of making light speed. In fact, it was right in the middle of that thought that Ghoulie's stomach dropped, his eyes blurred, and his ears filled with a *whoosh*.

5

Siege on Bot World

Up in the attic, Beamer saw a yellowish white light in the corner of his vision. He whirled around to see the web glowing like ... like—he couldn't think of anything it was like—maybe fairy dust. All he knew was that it meant the ship was taking off, and he wasn't on it!

"Wait!" he yelled as he scrambled out the window and fell in a roll down the roof to the tree. He clamored along the branches, jostling snow clods into pelting him with every frantic movement.

It momentarily occurred to him that he might see what the tree ship looked like when it warped away. *Of course, if the whole experience is only in my head, the tree ship isn't really going anywhere—or is it? Maybe the ship took them into another dimension.* Whatever it was, Beamer wanted to be *in* the ship, not watching it. "Wait!" he shouted with even more urgency.

Attack of the Spider Bots

Ghoulie looked out the cockpit window. The sky was now black with tiny sparkling dots. He looked down and noticed that he was wearing a red, yellow, and blue uniform with brass buttons. He'd gotten a promotion since their last jump — all the way to Captain.

The captain's eyes flared wide when he saw, directly in front of the ship, what looked like a large battleship floating sideways in space.

Ghoulie suddenly realized that Beamer and Scilla were nowhere to be seen. They'd been working outside the ship when it jumped. Fighting a growing sense of panic, he leaped from his seat and ran to the back of the ship. It took a strangely long time to get there. For one thing, the ship was growing longer right before his eyes. He knew that the bridge always seemed bigger than their little plywood cockpit, but he'd never been outside the bridge before. The ship didn't grow to be as big as Darth Vader's star destroyer, but it wasn't far from being as big as the Millennium Falcon or Princess Amidala's Naboo Royal Cruiser.

"Bruzelski ... MacIntyre! Where are you?" Captain Ives shouted into his communicator. "Report! Report!" he yelled again as he ran from compartment to compartment.

He got a blast of static and then heard, "We're coming in now, Captain. Opening air-lock door."

The captain then saw them outside the window, wearing bulky white suits and floating in space like birthday balloons. He sighed in relief as he watched them enter the air lock and saw the robotic arm next to them retract back into its compartment.

Minutes later, they were all together in the ship's bridge, staring at a space battleship on their view screen. Actually, it was bigger than a battleship. As they drew closer they began to see tall build-ings and needle spires growing out of its smooth, dark surface.

"It's a floating city!" exclaimed Commander MacIntyre.

"Not a favorite vacation spot, I think," said the captain wryly as he saw gashes and rubble where building walls should be.

"Not unless you're into digging through ruins," said Officer Bruzelski.

"Man! I hope we haven't dropped into the middle of a war," grumbled MacIntyre. "I'm fresh out of bravery pills."

"What do you think, Commander?" Captain Ives asked. "Warfare or a friendly visit from the neighborhood asteroid field?" Impact craters covered the surface of the space platform like it had been a shooting gallery. Through the craters, he could see a trash heap of what had once been buildings and streets beneath the surface. Whether the damage was from exploding bombs or just big rocks, the captain couldn't tell.

"Either way, she's totally gutted," said MacIntyre. "If she'd been on the sea instead of in space, she'd have sunk faster than the Titanic."

"Yeah," chimed in Bruzelski, "and probably crashed right into that planet."

In the lower left corner of the screen was an angry-looking planet. Not a very pleasant place, thought the commander. What he could see of the orange and black surface was pockmarked with erupting volcanoes. No question about it: only guys with pitch forks and red horns would feel comfortable down there.

"If it were to sink out of orbit, it wouldn't be to the planet," Captain Ives corrected them. "According to my readings, the floating city is following a cockeyed orbit around that ice-sheeted moon just above us."

Sure enough, just at the top of their view screen was the edge of a blue-white moon.

"How does a planet on fire get a frozen moon?" asked Bruzelski.

"Who knows? Maybe it's the hot planet's lollipop," quipped the commander, getting groans from the others in response. His expression suddenly morphed to high anxiety, and his fingers flew over his panel. "Captain, controls are no longer responding!" he shouted.

They flinched in unison as the speakers squawked with gibberish. "Hey!" yelled Bruzelski as she banged on the universal translator. Now they heard an automated voice speaking in another language, this one more familiar. "Whaddya think, maybe French?" she asked.

The captain came over and banged on the box several more times before they heard the announcement in English — well, English with an Australian accent.

The message, with lots of static and dropouts, announced: "G'day, mates. You are approaching terminal 847B. All attendants prepare for landing."

"Please stow your trays and return your seats to their upright position," Bruzelski said with a crooked smile as she held a mock microphone. "I guess it thinks we're the morning flight out of Chattanooga."

A moment later, the ship's engines shut off. "Uh ... Captain — " the commander said with a gulp.

Siege on Bot World

"MacIntyre," shouted the captain. "Reverse thrusters!"

The commander punched all the right dials and entered the proper commands, but —

"No response, Captain. They've got us in their tractor beam!" He gulped so hard he almost swallowed his Adam's apple as the floating, ruined city grew larger in their view screen.

"Officer Bruzelski," Captain Ives ordered. "Open all frequencies!"

"Aye, aye, Captain," she said as she adjusted her controls.

"Attention, space platform," announced the captain as if he were a TV announcer. "We do not wish to land at this time. We are just passing through." He paused and then added, "Nice to see you, though ... uh, hope you are doing well. Feel free to drop by when you are in our ... uh ... sector of the galaxy." He winced and gave the others a "whatever" shrug.

The only answer was more static.

The captain could see sets of trams and monorail trains skimming across the surface as they drew closer to the floating city ... and robots — lots of robots. The problem was he couldn't see any people.

It reminded the Ghoulie within the captain of Solomon Parker's train set, except that the space platform wasn't a toy and looked a lot more dangerous. Unfortunately, there was not a tree branch to be seen. They were lost in space!

Moments later — without so much as a bump — they were on the surface of the space platform. "Well, at least some things in this place work," said Bruzelski.

"Welcome to the International Peace Station," announced the speaker. "Please exit in an orderly manner and enjoy your visit."

"Some peace," said the captain. "Let's just hope they can't open the door remotely. I'd just as soon stay in an oxygen/nitrogen atmosphere."

Suddenly, machines near them on the platform started coming to life. Some ground immediately to a halt; others cast off showers of sparks; and still others took twisted courses toward their ship.

"Let's not panic now," ordered the captain, "but I suggest we put weapons on standby."

"Actually, I don't think we're under attack, sir," said Bruzelski. "See that? It looks like a fuel line. And those robots over there look like they're holding wrenches."

"Well, they might not be intentionally hostile," said the captain, "but they are not exactly in tip-top shape." He definitely had that right. Robots approached the ship, some limping on broken limbs, others spinning in circles on tracks instead of wheels. There were even some that looked fairly functional but just marched back and forth like tin soldiers. Every once in awhile, one stopped, as if its battery had run down. Then the ones behind it crashed into it and fell.

It would have been funny — like a tin-man version of the Keystone Cops — if the Star-Fighters had been watching it on TV instead of worrying that those walking cans might bang a hole in their ship.

"Duck!!" Bruzelski suddenly yelled as she hit the deck. A flying-saucer-shaped machine about the size of a serving plate zipped by. It had little eyes that peered menacingly at them. Another one suddenly spun into a dive and skimmed across the hull of the tree ship in a shower of sparks.

"Just what we need, kamikaze robots," grumbled MacIntyre. Officer Bruzelski picked herself up from the floor in time to hear something scratching at the window. Out the window, she could see what looked to be spiders about the size of her hand scrambling all over the hull. "Hey y'all," she said with a gulp, "we've got bugs — big ones with metal legs."

Actually, Scilla found them kind of cute, with their little bodies tilting up, down, and around mechanically, sputtering out oil and whirling their foot pads around to clean and polish their ship. It was particularly funny how they could squish down to the smallest size to clean in the cracks.

Then Officer Bruzelski heard the intruder alarm sounding within their ship. "Someone's triggered the air lock!" she cried as she jumped up and ran toward the bridge door. But she never got there. Squeezing out from beneath the door was a seemingly endless stream of spider bots!

6

Hide and Seek

"Help! Captain! We're being boarded!" cried Bruzelski as she began to swat the mechanical bugs. The good news was that the little buggers didn't squish into bug juice when she trounced on them. The bad news was that more spider bots kept coming.

Commander MacIntyre once again tried to fire the thrusters. "Still nothing, Captain," he shouted as he swiped a couple of the metal bugs off of his control panel.

The spider bots didn't look like they were trying to harm anybody. In fact, the control panel was shining and clean after they crawled across. Places on the floor were also showing a nice polish.

"Hey y'all, look at my hand," Bruzelski shouted as she shook a spider bot off. "It polished my nails!"

But just when they were ready to laugh, they noticed a wobbling spider bot moving across a wall, cutting out a slice as it moved. "Uh, oh, some of these guys

are out of wack too. Stop that!" cried Bruzelski, taking a broom
to the malfunctioning arachnid. "Yipe!" she yelped as another one
scrambled across her shoe, shaving off the front edge just in front
of her toe. Then it scrambled across a table and cut a groove
across the top. "Captain, these guys have lasers. We'd better do
something quick, or we're going to get sliced up like pastrami."

"MacIntyre, open fire!" ordered the captain.

"At what, the spider bots?" asked the frustrated commander.

"No ... at everything outside!" Captain Ives yelled. "We have to
deactivate the tractor beam that pulled us onto the space platform.
The control transmitter has to be out there somewhere!"

The commander shrugged and started shooting all the ship's
weapons at once, including the veton depth charges and the stickeyon
emissions. With the gravitation field of the space platform no longer
functioning, the stickeyon emission traveled much farther than usual.
That sticky substance must have gummed up a rotating radio control
transmitter because everything ground to a stop, including the spider
bots. Even better, whatever was pinning the ship to that platform was
also shut off.

"We're on our own power!" cried MacIntyre. He gunned the
thrusters, and they took off.

They were no sooner back in space than they suddenly found
themselves back in the tree.

"It's about time!" sputtered Scilla, erupting from beneath
a cluster of disabled spider bots. Her uniform was in tatters.
"I was within seconds of becoming human confetti." At that
moment, her uniform transformed once again into jeans,

sweater, and an overcoat. She looked down at the spider bots. They had turned into piles of twigs and shirt buttons.

"I'm just glad the ship is still in one piece," said Ghoulie with a huge sigh. He fingered a burn streak across one corner of a plywood table. "Do you ever wonder how much of our adventures might be real?" he asked thoughtfully.

"Like if that space platform is really out in space some-where?" Beamer echoed his thoughts.

"Come on, y'all," said Scilla with a twisted grin. "Do you really think we could be whisked to the farthest edge of space in the blink of an eye? Not possible. Hey, Mr. Spock," she said to Ghoulie. "Come on, where's your science?"

"Of course, you're right," he said, shaking his head as if to clear his mind. "It's just that it always seems so real. After all, it wasn't our imagination that sliced through this table."

"Whether it's real or not, I wish we knew what happened to that space platform," said Beamer. "I mean, if it was attacked or bombarded by asteroids, why didn't anybody bother to fix it? Did they all die or just give up?"

That night, while he was staring up at the water-stained ceiling above his bed, the idea of giving up rolled around in Beamer's head like a loose marble. He was thinking that it was about time to do just that with his baseball career. The season was long over, of course, but soon he'd have to make a decision about the next season. It wasn't like he'd had this big dream of becoming a major league star.

Among the ranks of little league baseball players, he was a fairly decent pitcher. But when it came to batting, all he ever hit was air. *Why can't I get the stupid bat to go where my eyes tell me it's supposed to go?* His dad had told him about "eye-hand coordination"—that some kids got it earlier than others. But that didn't help much when the guy wearing a bag on his chest shouted, "Strike three!" Beamer remembered how, after his last time at bat in the championship game, the umpire had jerked his arm back like he was cocking a rifle. *Talk about rubbing it in. Where did that ump think he was, Yankee Stadium?*

But the worst moment came when he heard a rasping chuckle behind him. He looked over to see Jared watching him through the chain-link fence. Jared had stopped being a direct threat to the Star-Fighters, thanks to that little battle in the tree last fall. Nor could he any longer get away with fleecing kids at school of their milk money. Still, Beamer knew that this underage Terminator was aching to return to the top of the middle-school food chain.

On that day, though, Jared wasn't using his fists. He was using his bat to intimidate everyone. He was a year older than Beamer, but they were in the same division. And while Beamer was fanning away, his cud-chewing nemesis had the highest batting average and the most home runs in the league. How was Beamer supposed to compete if his brain and his reflexes wouldn't cooperate? So why not just give up? Besides, if he didn't compete, he couldn't lose. Right?

* * * * *

The next morning, Middle America got hit by another snow storm, and Beamer was forced to wear his snow boots again. As he pulled them out from the closet, he noticed something stuck to the bottom of one of the boots. It was an old piece of paper—old as in ancient Egyptian papyrus—dull yellow-brown and extra crispy. The huge wad of bubble gum that glued it to the tread was also holding the paper together, since it was cracked into about a million pieces.

Beamer hadn't worn the boots since they had visited the old trolley terminal. Sure enough, the paper was a memo from the trolley company. It announced a farewell party being held at the company president's house—Solomon Parker's house! The address was in more pieces than anything else, but he could pick out the street name: "onial." He made a copy of the bottom of the boot on the family's all-in-one printer/copier, in case the note fell apart when he tried to remove it. Then he taped the gummy note together and carefully pried it off, hoping the tape would hold it together.

He'd never heard of an Onial street. Later that day, Beamer got Ghoulie and Scilla to check out all the maps they could find. But no luck—no Onial. Even Mr. Parker's *street* had dropped off the planet. He still had the copy of the note in his hand at dinnertime when his mom plopped down a plate full of meat loaf, peas, and macaroni.

"What do you have there?" she asked Beamer as she returned to the kitchen. "Uhven two at twenty pahcent; uhven wun, awf," he heard her say. She'd been getting better at talking to the appliances. Practically nothing in the house worked unless you talked to it—not just in English, but in a Southern accent. His mother, who was usually called Dr. Mac by her kiddie patients, came back in with two more plates. She then looked over Beamer's shoulder at the paper. "What is that a copy of? Looks pretty old," she said, seeing all the cracks in the note. "Where'd you get it?"

Suddenly there was a screech and a whisk of wind as Beamer's little brother, Michael, flew around the table and ripped the note out of his hand. "Got it!" he chortled. "The treasure is mine!"

Beamer was on him in an instant. "Give that back, noodle brain; it's not a treasure map!" Before Michael could uncross his eyes from trying to read the note, Beamer had it back. "It's a memo with the address to Old Lady Parker's brother's house."

"Beamer!" said his mother through tight lips, with her hands on her hips. "It's not respectful to refer to someone as 'Old Lady.'"

"Sorry, Mom," he said with a guilty look. "It's just that I can't find Mr. Parker's street name on any map."

"Here, let me have a look," she said, wiping her hands on her apron. She took the note as Beamer propped his elbows on either side of his plate and dropped his head into his hands.

"This is a Xerox of your boot?" she asked incredulously. "Where's the str—?" she started. "Oh, I see—onial." She suddenly laughed. "Onial's only part of the name, honey. I'd put my bet on the name being Colonial. There's a Colonial Street just a few blocks away."

* * * * *

That's how Beamer, Ghoulie, and Scilla found themselves standing in the middle of Colonial Street a few days later. Ghoulie had wondered how they'd find the house without a street number, but that turned out not to be a problem. The houses down one side of the street were no bigger than Beamer's house. There was only one house on the other side of the street. At least they figured a house was there some-where. All they could see was a wall high enough to hold back King Kong. Whether it was made of brick or stone or Lego blocks, they couldn't tell, for it was completely cov-ered with a thick layer of vines. And on top of the vines was a heavy coat of snow. Frankly, if the gate hadn't been set between two towers, they wouldn't have known where it was. The gate was, however, firmly locked.

"Now what?" muttered Scilla. "It might be easier to get into Fort Knox."

"There's got to be a calling thingy here somewhere," Ghoulie said as he started shuffling through the vines on the left tower.

"Maybe the place is too old for stuff like that," said Scilla as she tried shaking the huge iron gate. A snow clod the size of a beach ball immediately fell and plastered her from ponytail to galoshes.

"Great!" she said as she wiped a handful of snow from each eye. She shed more snow as she turned toward Beamer and Ghoulie, who were snickering like a couple of hyenas with the hiccups. She cocked her hip, throwing off still more snow, and gave them a slow burn. A moment later her gaze lifted to a spot on the gate tower behind them. "When you're through polluting the sound waves, you can push that button behind you."

The boys twisted their heads around and saw the message console only partly cluttered with vines. Beamer reached up and pushed a button. "Hello ... uh ... my name is Beamer MacIntyre, and I'm one of the Star-Fighters—"

Above the button was a small TV screen. It was blank, but they heard a snooty, feminine recorded voice say, "We are not receiving unsolicited visitors at this time. However, if you have a visitor's pass, please enter your code now."

"I repeat," said Scilla to her buddies, once again cocking her hip, "now what?"

"The lady on the speaker doesn't sound very friendly to me," said Ghoulie. "I say we forget Mr. Parker, especially since everybody else seems to have forgotten him."

"You're probably right," said Beamer with a sigh. He kicked a rock into the street, walked up to it, and kicked it again to the other side of the street.

"We've got better things to do than chase down people who don't want to be caught," Ghoulie added as he followed Beamer across the street.

Suddenly the speaker croaked, and a very weak, breathy voice said, "Is somebody there? Who did you say you were?"

7
Lost in the Jungle

"Wait!" Beamer cried as he ran back across the street. He caught the slightest grainy glimpse of an old man's face on the TV screen before it went blank. He pushed the button again and said, "We are the Star-Fighters ... from Murphy Street—" The speaker squealed loudly, causing all three kids to hold their ears in pain. Then the speaker was silent. Beamer banged the button hard and said, "Hello, is anyone there? Is that you, Mr. Parker?" This time there was no answer.

Beamer started pacing back and forth in front of the gate.

"Take it easy, Beamer," said Scilla. "You'll wear a hole in the sidewalk."

"Something's wrong," he said. "We have to get in there." He charged the wall and leaped onto the vines, trying to pull himself up. He kept sliding back down as one vine after another shredded beneath his weight. He finally gave up and sat on the sidewalk with his chin in his hands.

"You … Tarzan," said Ghoulie, mimicking the deep, staccato way Tarzan spoke in the old movies. "No swing on vines in Middle America."

Beamer's attention, however, was focused down the street. "Come on!" he said suddenly and scrambled toward a tree that had grown up next to the street. "What do you think you're going to do?" asked Ghoulie as he and Scilla chased after him. "That tree's a good seven feet from the wall. Unless you've got wings or a rocket backpack, you'll never be able to jump that far."

Beamer wasn't even sure the tree would hold him; it was tall, but its branches were very thin. In fact, the tree shook as he started climbing, shedding what little snow it held like a white cloud.

"Beamer—" Scilla shouted, "you'll break your stupid neck trying to get to that stupid wall from that stupid tree!"

Beamer kept on climbing. In fact, he kept on climbing even when he passed the height of the wall.

"Beamer!" both Ghoulie and Scilla kept yelling at him.

The tree was now teetering back and forth from his weight on a high branch. It was a little scary, but that is what Beamer wanted it to do. Finally, the tree swung over far enough for him to kick at the snow pack atop the wall. But it wasn't far enough for him to leap onto the wall. So he sidled up the tree to a higher and even more feeble branch and tried again. Once more he swung out over the wall. He was feeling pretty good about himself. One more second and he'd just drop onto the wall. But then he heard a loud *crack*, and his stomach jumped into his throat. The branch had broken! He was falling!

Suddenly he stopped with a harsh jerk. With his heartbeat up around 100 beats per second, Beamer opened his eyes to see that he was dangling high over the sidewalk, like a gymnast holding on to a high bar. He looked over to see that the far end of the branch had fallen onto the wall, while the broken end had lodged into a *V* between two lower branches.

"Beamer!" both of his friends cried together. "Are you all right? Beamer?"

His arms felt like stretched-out bubble gum. He smiled weakly to his buddies below and said in a high-pitched whimper, "Well, I've found a way in."

Beamer slowly pulled himself across the branch to the wall while Ghoulie and Scilla reluctantly followed his route. After much complaining and grumbling, they all huddled at the foot of the wall inside Mr. Parker's yard.

The bad news was they still couldn't see the house. The other bad news was the yard was more of a jungle than a yard.

"Are we still in Middle America?" Scilla asked.

"If not, we're on a very unfriendly planet," said Beamer with a gulp.

It had been so long since anyone had mowed the yard that there wasn't anything left to mow. The trees planted long ago had become a forest. The weeds had grown into heavy brush and thin, spidery trees which wild vines wound around like boa constrictors. You couldn't stroll through this forest; you had to climb through it.

"What if he's got guard dogs or—" Scilla whispered.

"Laser guns or SWAT teams?" Ghoulie finished for her.

"Who needs guard dogs when you have a jungle guarding the way?" said Beamer with a lump growing in his throat. The coating of snow made it look all the more eerie. Instead of magical, the winter here seemed bleak and threatening. "We might oughta throw out a few heavy-duty prayers." He was sure he saw one of the winding vines move. *Do snakes come out in the winter?*

"Well, might as well get eaten on the run as stay sittin' here waiting to be surrounded," Scilla finally said with a hard swallow. "It can't be too far to the house. This block's not that big."

They made their way slowly through the brush, crawling and climbing around and through the tangle of vines, weeds, and twisted trees. Eyes wide, they listened for the sound of snarling dogs or for anything slithering or hissing. What made things worse was that they kept having to stop to untangle their clothes from snags and thorns. Just when Beamer was sure they were going in circles, they finally glimpsed the roof of a house.

"Okay, what are we supposed to do now?" asked Scilla through the corner of her mouth. "Knock on the door and say howdy?"

"Yeah, what's the plan, Beamer?" Ghoulie asked as he hunched down beside him.

"It took all the plannin' I had in me to get over the wall," said Beamer. "It's your turn now."

"My turn? You're the guy who's been so hot to find Mr. Parker. So go find him."

That's when the storm troopers arrived, or storm buggers ... or whatever. A whirring sound filled the trees all around them like a swarm of locusts. The next thing they knew, the spindly branches high in the trees seemed to be falling down on top of them. Then those spidery branches started spreading out in groups of eight, each group suspended beneath a central pod. Before the kids could run out of the way, they were each in a kind of birdcage created by a surrounding set of eight tall legs.

"They are *spiders*," screamed Scilla on the verge of panic. "Giant, long-legged spiders!"

8
Dragon Lady

"Do not move," several metallic voices said in perfect unison, "and you will not be harmed."

The voices came from the central pod, or body, of each spider, which was propped up on legs that were about twice as tall as the kids.

"They're mechanical spiders," said a wide-eyed Scilla.

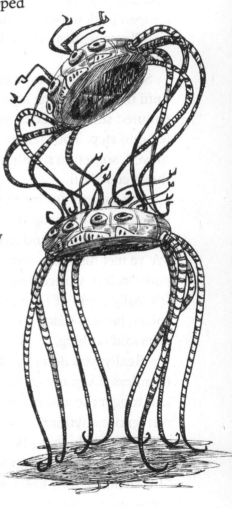

The pods were dome-topped metal cylinders about the size of large trash cans with rivets all over them. There were four eyes spread evenly around each pod at the base of the dome. By itself, the pod looked something like the old robots Beamer had seen pictures of from back in the 1930s and 40s.

"Long legs and a small body," said Ghoulie. "Better that than the other way around."

"They're like giant daddy longlegs," said Beamer.

"Yeah, and daddy longlegs aren't dangerous," said Ghoulie.

"Let's hope these dudes aren't either," added Scilla.

Suddenly two legs from one of the creatures folded at the joints and clasped Scilla. "Eiiiiiiiii!" she screamed in a pitch that probably broke every glass within a mile. But all the creature did was scoot her more securely within its encircling set of spindly legs. "Let me go, you oversized bag of stilts!" she shouted and tried to escape by squeezing between the legs. The legs, however, gave her a small electric shock, and she jumped back into the middle.

"Please walk as we walk," the creatures said as with one voice.

Scilla, being the especially stubborn sort, refused to move until the beast's back legs shocked her into moving. She endured several shocks, yelping each time, before she finally fell into step. The creatures clanked mechanically as they moved, sometimes with squealing and scraping sounds, as if they needed oil.

"We weren't just breaking in, you know," Beamer said nervously to their captors. "I mean, we don't do that sort of thing—vandalism and stuff. We just wanted to see Mr. Parker. We've met his sister—you know, the one in the Castle near the park. In fact, we accidentally found his train set the other day. It's really cool." If Beamer hoped to charm the mechanical spider, he was mistaken. The creature in the hard jacket on stilts said nothing.

"Really, you don't need to worry about us. We're totally harmless. Even my mom thinks so, except when I track in dirt and trigger the automatic vacuum into going nuts. And you can ignore anything my sister says about me. She's certifiable." The only thing Beamer heard was the clanking of the mechanical stilts. His abductor was clearly the silent type. "Incidentally, they know where we are—sort of. So, if I'm not home for dinner, you could get into a lot of trouble."

"Hey, I bet you'd like my tree house. It's shaped like a spaceship. Nobody ever believes us when we talk about it, but it's really kind of magical. We get to go all over the—"

Beamer received an electrical shock as he tripped over the driveway. Cracked and overgrown with weeds, it circled a large water fountain that looked like it hadn't been spouting water since soon after the invention of plumbing. The far side of the driveway skirted a broad porch lined with tall columns. Something about the columns didn't look right to Beamer. He tilted his head and studied them more carefully ... until the back legs of his prison shocked him into walking faster. By then, though, he had figured out that the columns were set at an angle, running from a wide circle on the porch floor to a smaller circle beneath a balcony above the double front door.

That balcony was also pretty strange looking. You see, the house had a dome. Beamer thought that domes were supposed to be on top of buildings, but this one stuck out the front of the house like a pimple. The balcony was cut out of the bottom of that sideways dome. Just above the balcony, in the center of the dome, was a big round window. Suddenly, the picture clicked in Beamer's head. "Hey, guys!" he whispered too loudly. "It's a train! The whole front of the house is shaped like a streamlined locomotive!"

Suddenly a woman stepped onto the porch and winced in the bright sunlight. She wasn't smiling. Actually, she had a long, lean faced that looked like it hadn't smiled for an eon or two. The good news for her was that her face had no laugh lines. The bad news was that she had loads of frown lines.

"Hello, children," she said in a high-pitched, whining voice. "I am Mrs. Drummond, and I'm sure I don't need to tell you that I could turn you over to the police for trespassing." She tilted her face down to look through the upper part of her bifocals.

"As you can see we have gone to a great deal of trouble to maintain our privacy." Tall and wiry, she wore a long, dark dress with almost no decorations, except for puffed up shoulders. Her hair was piled up in a ring on top of her head, which was held up by a long, narrow neck, reminding Beamer of those aliens you'd see in movies who had big heads tilting and turning on tiny necks.

"However, I am going to overlook your actions this time. But I warn you against repeating this intrusion. Mr. Parker is very ill. He was once a very brilliant man, as you can see from these sentry creatures he constructed long ago. Incidentally, I must ask that you tell no one of the existence of these creatures. Mr. Parker's health is very fragile, and any undue excitement can pose a danger to him," she added with a cold smile.

Beamer felt his face flush at the same time a chill spread down toward his feet. It hadn't occurred to him that they might endanger the man's health by dropping by.

She glanced up at the sentries and ordered, "See that these children leave the premises and then return to your posts." Without another glance at the kids, she turned around and reentered the house.

Something about the way she whirled around, her head turning slower than her body like a snake pivoting about, with her arms lifted high in a gesture of dismissal, gave Beamer the brief image of a dragon with its wings spread, guarding a cave full of treasure.

*   *   *   *   *

About half an hour later Beamer closed his front door and turned to find a sword pointed at his chest.

"Do you yield?" a guy wearing a mask and armor asked in a gruff voice.

"Yes, Dad, I yield," Beamer said with a sigh, pushing the plastic sword away with his finger. Why couldn't he have a normal dad—you know, just some everyday SWAT team member or a spy for the CIA? Nope, his dad was the king of make-believe—a theater director at the local college. Naturally, he had to try out the props for each new theater production at home. Beamer had a feeling that his dad would play every part himself if he could get away with it. But then, on the positive side, his half-kid father could often make sense of what made no sense to Beamer.

While his father continued his duel with an invisible opponent, Beamer told him about his experience with Mr. Parker and Mrs. Drummond.

"Sounds like there is nothing you can do," his father said as he put down the sword and took off his mask.

"Something doesn't sound right, though," Beamer said with a stiff jaw.

"Yes, but as unpleasant as the lady seems to be, she knows more about Mr. Parker's health than you do. Now leave them alone. It is far too dangerous to pursue Mr. Parker's situation any further. Oh," he said, changing the subject at the same time he was changing into a helmet with bull horns sticking out on each side. "Your mother and I contacted Social Services about the boy in the trolley station. They've apparently known about him for some time but have never been able to find him." He picked up a rubber battle axe and swung it around. "Can you imagine that?" he asked as Beamer ducked. "They said that they would try again—maybe bring in the police."

9

Never-Never Land

"What are we doing here?" protested Scilla, huffing and puffing behind Beamer as they approached the trolley terminal turned ice Castle. "You got your wallet back."

"Do you want the kid picked up by the police?" he countered her.

They went into the building. Everything inside was linked together in rolling hills of snow. With every step came a *crunch*. They could forget about sneaking up on the little crook.

"Why didn't Ghoulie come?" Scilla asked.

"His parents were taking him out to an amusement park for their anniversary," Beamer said as he huffed clouds of chilled breath into the station. He banged through the side door, and they were once again in the trolley-car graveyard.

"Is this the right car?" he asked Scilla when he reached the trolley-car door where he thought they'd found the thief's stuff last time.

"Pretty sure," she answered as she jumped up to the first step. "I remember that the car next to it had a broken window and a twisted mirror the same as it has now."

"Yeah, well, something's definitely not the same here." The trolley was empty. It was like the kid had never been there. He'd left nothing behind—no clothes, no gadgets, no loot—nothing. "As they say, he's gone without a trace," said Beamer.

They went on to search the other trolley cars. This time, though, they skipped the ones that required jumping up to see through the windows. If they couldn't get inside, the chances were the little hobo couldn't either, and Beamer didn't want another headache.

"Come on," Beamer said as he started walking back to the station. "We may as well look for the *ghost* of Mr. Parker while we're here."

"Ghost?" exclaimed Scilla. "You didn't say anything about a ghost."

"It's sort of his ghost—we're looking for what Mr. Parker left behind when he disappeared."

"Cute, MacIntyre," said Scilla with a crooked grin.

They finally found the station office on a balcony above the passenger and ticketing area. It wasn't a pretty sight. Someone had treated the place like it was the city dump. Drawers had been broken out of the desks and filing cabinets. A confetti factory wouldn't have had as much paper strewn about.

"I'll take what's left of the filing cabinets," said Scilla.

Beamer started going through desk and table drawers. "Doesn't look promising," Beamer said as a drawer broke apart and crashed to the floor.

"Maybe there's more here than you'd think," Scilla said as she plopped to the ground beneath the weight of a huge file folder. "There's a bunch of newspaper clippings still here—really old ones." Scilla picked up the first one only to have it immediately crumble to pieces in her hand. "Whoa," she said and laid the folder flat on the floor between her crossed legs. She leaned over the folder and turned the next page like it was made of thin glass. "Here's a picture of the trolley station under construction, and here's another one of trolley tracks being laid."

Beamer slid down beside her. A newspaper photo showed a man getting an award from a city official. Beamer started to grab it, but Scilla shook him off. "Take it easy. These are halfway to dust already."

"Okay, but then what's it say?" he asked impatiently.

"This one says somethin' about going into bankruptcy," she said.

"That's pretty bad," mumbled Beamer.

"Sounds like the trolley business didn't make any money," said Scilla. "Too bad Ghoulie's not here—numbers bein' his thing and all."

"Happened back in 1951," said Beamer as he pointed at the date.

They suddenly heard a *thump* above their heads. "Someone's on the roof!" Beamer exclaimed as he jumped up. He ran out the door, then suddenly reappeared, twisting around to look back in at Scilla. "Bring that stuff with you. We'll get Ghoulie to go over it with us back at the tree ship."

"You got any idea how heavy this thing is?" Scilla yelled after him. But he was already gone. Scilla rolled her eyes, muttering, "Boys talk, girls get things done," as she carefully folded everything back up.

A moment later Beamer was outside the station. He spun around to look at the roof just in time to get his breath knocked out. He fell back into a small snowdrift with a football planted on his chest.

"Hey, nice catch!" yelled the boy, laughing on the rooftop like a rooster.

"Hey, where have you been hiding?" Beamer yelled back

at him. "We've been looking for you everywhere."

"You and Social Services," he said with a disgruntled look. "Why'd you rat me out for?"

"Whaddya mean, rat you out? It's dangerous being here by yourself in the middle of winter. You could freeze to death or starve or get mugged or—"

"Hey, old Jack can take care of himself. I've been doin' it for a couple years now, ever since my dad died and my mom flipped out on drugs. Come on, throw me the ball," he ordered.

The boy—Jack—spoke with a drawl like Scilla but with a little country-western flair. Beamer stood up awkwardly and threw a wobbling pass back to him. "Where'd you get the football, anyway? Steal it?"

"Look here," he answered with a sudden hard look. "Jack's no thief. I only take what other folks lose or throw away. You wouldn't believe what they toss out—especially the rich folk."

"What about my wallet, huh?" Beamer asked with a cocky look. "I didn't just 'lose' it."

"Hey, I was gonna pay ya back. In fact, I've got it right here." He threw what looked like a little ball at Beamer's feet. "Just consider it a little investment."

Beamer picked up the object and discovered that it was a few dollar bills wrapped around a rock and held together by rubber bands.

That's when Scilla came running out of the station awkwardly carrying a half-torn paper box that bumped against her body. "Whatcha got?" she asked.

"The money he stole from me," said Beamer, pointing at the boy on the roof as he examined the ball of money, "and one dollar more."

Scilla turned and shielded her eyes against the bright snow to see him, dropping the box in the process.

"All right, *go long*," Jack yelled at Beamer, waving the

football in the air.

"Wait, I'm—" Beamer protested as he started to backpedal.

"No, the other way," Jack yelled. "Come on, I said *long!*"

Beamer ran, slipping and sliding across the snow and ice. Jack heaved the ball in an almost perfect spiral. Beamer stretched out to catch it and fell onto the ice. Amazingly, especially to himself, he still managed to hold on to the ball as he slid on his belly.

Jack leaped off the roof like Peter Pan in a wintry Never-Never Land. "Way to go, what's your face—nice catch!" Jack yelled. He leaped up, cocking his arms like a pro player on TV, or maybe a rooster on Animal Planet.

Scilla ran over to see if Beamer was all right, but he waved her off. "My name is not what's your face," Beamer grumbled after he spit out a mouth full of snow. "It's Beamer, Beamer MacIntyre."

"Okay, Beamer," Jack said agreeably. But then he stopped to think about it. "You sure it's Beamer? I've never heard of anythin' besides a car called a Beamer."

"I am not 'a Beamer,' just Beamer, and I've never heard of anybody who lived in a trolley car either," Beamer threw back at him.

"Hey, it beats being locked up in some government joint. Here I've got my freedom and a pretty cool playground. Now tell the little guy next to you to go out for a pass."

"I'm not a guy!" Scilla said in a huff as she whipped off her stocking cap to reveal her dark blonde ponytail. "The name's Scilla."

"Oh, sorry," said Jack with a grimace. "Here, kid ... uh ... Beamer. Hit me over middle." He was just starting to run when Scilla cut in front of him.

"Hey, what do y'all think you're doing?" she shouted at Jack. "Just because I'm a girl, doesn't mean I can't play football. Come on, Beamer, I'm gonna cut right." She ran about ten strides and then cut right. Beamer lofted the ball but it wobbled away behind her.

"Whoa there, Beamer," Jack said as he ran to scoop up the ball. "Your passing technique's strictly in the toilet. Here, let me show ya," he said as he walked toward Beamer, tossing the ball up and down several times.

He worked like a coach showing Beamer the way to hold the ball, until Beamer's passes started losing their wobble. Surprisingly enough, they all started having fun, catching and passing or trying to block or intercept. They plopped and skidded, getting face-fulls of snow and throwing alley-oop passes over the trolley cars. By the time the sun was low in the sky, they were so caked in snow they could have passed for gingerbread cookies—iced.

"Hey, we gotta get goin'," Scilla finally said. "My grandma doesn't even know where I am. If she start's worrying, I could be in big doo-doo."

"Me too," chimed in Beamer.

Jack looked disappointed, and his eyes started moving like he was thinking up something. "Well, y'all are about the worst football players I've ever seen," he finally said with his rooster laugh, "but I can work you into shape. When y'all comin' back?"

They looked at each other and shrugged almost at the same time. "I don't know," Beamer mumbled. "We're not supposed to be here at all." After an awkward silence, he shrugged again and said, "We'll see what we can do. Where can we find you?"

"Nice try, Beamer," Jack said with a smirk. "I'll find y'all, but only if y'all are alone."

10

The House that Time Forgot

That night Beamer had to face some heavy-duty interrogation. Luckily his parents weren't into thumbscrews and electric shocks. When the questioning was over, it was torture enough that they forced him to clean up his room. Brushing the dust off his wall-length Lego monorail system took him a whole hour! "Cleanliness is next to godliness," they'd always say, as if it was in the Bible or something. Frankly, as far as Beamer was concerned, cleanliness was way overrated. Nobody ever had to sweep the forest floor or dust the rocks on a mountain.

Well, the Star-Fighters did have to dust the instrument panels in the tree ship from time to time. Otherwise, they couldn't read them. But that was a definite exception. In fact, it was while they were polishing things up a few days later that the crew got their first airmail delivery. Beamer heard it bang off the side of the tree ship.

Attack of the Spider Bots

Beamer ran out the door and picked it up off the outside platform. It was another wad of paper wrapped around a rock with rubber bands. "Hey, Jack!" he yelled down toward the ground. "Are you down there?"

"Nope, jus' me," yelled Beamer's little brother. "Who's Jack? Anyway, some man in a fancy suit delivered this to the house a few minutes ago. Dad asked me to give it to you, and this seemed the fastest way to do it."

"Thanks a lot, bubble brain," Beamer grumbled. "I can hardly read this wrinkled wad of trash. At least try using a Frisbee next time." Beamer smoothed the paper out enough to read the typed message beneath an elegant letterhead. "Hey guys," he yelled to the others inside. "You won't believe this!"

Seconds later, Ghoulie and Scilla crowded up next to him over the message. Beamer read it out loud: "Mr. Parker requests the presence of the Star-Fighters at his home at #2455 Colonial Street this coming Saturday at 2:00. Please be mindful of Mr. Parker's condition and prepare to act with respect and the utmost courtesy." Beamer folded up the message neatly.

They looked at each other in amazement. Finally Scilla said, "Judgin' from the last sentence, I'd say it was Mrs. Drummond who wrote it, and she's not overjoyed with the idea."

"Well, at least she gave us a code number to input at the gate," said Ghoulie.

* * * * *

On Saturday, the Star-Fighters appeared at 2:00 sharp and were dressed just as sharply. Scilla even wore a dress. Beamer and Ghoulie almost didn't recognize her. She couldn't stop wiggling and pulling the hem down to cover her spindly legs.

Ghoulie's mom drove them to the gate and flooded them with a thousand dos and don'ts. You'd have thought they were going to the White House. Ghoulie plugged in the code, and

68

the gate opened obediently, though with a lot of grating and squealing. They waved good-bye to Ghoulie's mom as the gate closed behind them, and they turned to walk up the lonely, broken driveway.

Mrs. Drummond met them at the door, her face as dark as a storm cloud. "Follow me," she said like a drill sergeant, "and keep your hands to yourself." Scilla saw Beamer open his mouth to speak. "And no talking," she added. His mouth snapped shut.

The house was the closest thing to a palace Scilla had ever seen. The entry room was as big as a hotel lobby. Grand doorways bordered by columns led to rooms on either side of the large room. Mrs. Drummond led them straight ahead, beneath a double staircase that circled from either side of the entry room to a second-story entry above. Everything was polished and gleaming, but the house still seemed dark and old—as in Dark Ages old. Scilla looked around for a suit of armor—one with moving eyes and a sword ready to lop off somebody's head.

As they walked down the wide hallway, Scilla sensed something familiar about the house. It took her awhile, since she'd never been in a house this grand, but then it hit her. The furniture, curtains, decorations, the figurines, and pictures were like what you'd find in any older woman's house—and Scilla had been with her grandmother to many such homes. As they moved toward the back of the house, Scilla looked into one room after another. There were no big chairs, no heavy cabinets or tables, but lots of glass cabinets filled with delicate figurines. But this was supposed to be a man's house—Mr. Parker's house!

Mrs. Drummond took them up a narrow flight of stairs at the back of the house. Upstairs was a whole different world.

Here were long carved tables, huge stuffed chairs and sofas, large grandfather clocks, and heavy carved bookcases. Here was a man's world—but a much-abandoned man's world. Nothing was out of place, but the dust on the floor, rugs, and furniture was as thick as turkey gravy. Windows were so covered with grime, you couldn't even see out.

Even worse were the spiderwebs. They were in the corners of every door and entryway, winding through and around the furniture like superhighways. Strangely, the webs were the brightest objects in the rooms. Their delicate designs provided the only thing close to beauty among the ruins.

Mrs. Drummond finally stopped before a large set of heavily carved double-doors. She turned back to the Star-Fighters with a dour look. "I am going to open these doors, but you are not to step into the room. Nor are you to utter a single word. Do you understand?" She waited until they had all nodded their heads before she turned and opened the doors.

The room behind the doors was the largest Scilla had ever seen outside of a movie. It was also brighter than the other rooms. That was because the curved wall on the far side of the room was lined with tall, arched windows. Once upon a time this might have been a beautiful ballroom, like in *Beauty and the Beast*. But that mood was ruined by the large ghostly objects which were spread about the room like mountainous islands in a sea of marble. You couldn't tell what they were because they were covered with milky plastic sheets, which is why they all looked so ghostly.

Scilla almost missed seeing the object next to the windows. At first it looked like a small square on wheels, but as Scilla's eyes adjusted to the light, she could see that it was a white-haired man in a wheelchair.

"That is Mr. Parker," the woman said. "He has spent his

days in that same place, looking out those same windows, for nearly fifty years." Mrs. Drummond took a deep breath. "Now, if you will follow me quietly, I will introduce you to him. No running around, shouting, or screaming, or I will pull you out of here by your ears. Is that understood?" she added through clenched teeth and in a voice as harsh as gravel. She glared at them as if hoping they would give her an excuse to throw them out right then. The kids, however, nodded sheepishly, their lips tightly sealed.

The covered objects loomed over them as she wove a path through the room. Making them look even more ominous was the network of cobwebs that connected them. Scilla could almost feel her skin crawl when she ducked beneath a web and stood back up to see a huge object with long arms (or claws or pinchers) that stretched over her head. She clamped her eyes closed, expecting to be snatched up and cut in two. That's when she bumped into Ghoulie who yelped in fright. Mrs. Drummond wheeled around so quickly they felt a gust of wind. "What was that?" she asked, glaring at them so hard that Scilla thought her red eyes were going to pop out. Then she heard another voice.

11

The Ghost of a Dream

"Mrs. Drummond," the words sounded breathy and crackling. "Are those the children you have with you?"

She held their gaze a moment longer before turning toward the old man. "Yes, Mr. Parker, I have them right here. I urge you to reconsider your decision. These children are particularly unruly and lacking in discipline. I am afraid their presence will only upset you—"

"That is quite all right, Mrs. Drummond," he said. "A little noise will probably be good for me after all these years."

"That is total nonsense," she responded with a temper. She quickly caught herself, though, and spoke more gently. "If you will permit me, I will be happy to stay here with you and make sure that they do not misbehave—"

"No, no, I appreciate your concern, but I want to speak with them alone. I will call you when they are ready to leave. Thank you very kindly, Mrs. Drummond."

"Yes sir," she said, nodding her head. Then she turned and walked back across the room.

"Please close the door behind you, if you will, Mrs. Drummond," the old man said as he turned his wheelchair around and faced her.

"Yes sir," she responded again, holding them in a murderous stare until the door closed across her bloodshot eyes.

Mr. Parker turned back to the kids. "So you are the children who are playing in the tree house these days?" The old man looked at all three of them in turn.

"Yes, sir, uh-huh," Beamer and Ghoulie answered. Scilla just nodded her head.

"I don't entertain guests often. Actually, it's been something like thirty years, maybe more. I can't remember." He spoke the words as if they required a great deal of effort. For a moment his eyes held a faraway look. Then he snapped out of it and said, "I don't know what kids drink these days ..." He pointed a shaking finger toward a small table where several glasses and a pitcher were neatly arranged. "I asked Mrs. Drummond to make some lemonade. I couldn't imagine that kids would ever stop loving lemonade. Please help yourselves."

The three quickly picked up glasses already half-full of lemonade. "Thank you, Mr. Parker," each said one on top of the other.

"No, no, call me Sol ... please."

Solomon Parker didn't have as many wrinkles as his sister, thought Beamer, *but then nobody did. He wasn't as big as she was either. He looked kind of frail, in fact, and sad, and moved as if his head and arms were almost unbearably heavy.*

"I heard about the tree house," he said. "Never got to play in it myself," he added with a note of bitterness. "My big sister didn't like the kid who built it—let's see, I believe his name was ... uh ... Stoll ... something."

"Billy Stoller," Ghoulie corrected him.

"Yes, that's right. Anyway," he went on as if the words tasted like sour lemons, "Rebecca convinced my parents that playing in the tree house was dangerous, so they wouldn't allow it."

Rebecca? Oh ... right ... Old Lady Parker's first name—the "R" of the "R.I.P." initials written on the walls of the caves beneath her house, remembered Beamer. *Of course, considering the adventures we've been on so far, she might have been right. None of us has ever been hurt, but we've sure gotten our hearts pumping. But then, if those adrenalin juices didn't get flowing, you probably couldn't call it an adventure.*

"I consider that one of the greatest regrets of my life," the old man said with a grim smile. "Oh, I am sorry if my robots frightened you on your last visit. My assistant, Mrs. Drummond, insists on such security measures. I designed them, of course ... years ago," he said, his voice fading as if he was reaching far back in time again. A moment later he popped back to the present and said, "Her job, though, is to ... uh, keep the bills paid and ... provide for the household needs. So, naturally, she wants to keep everything ... safe. Frankly, I can't imagine what I could have that anyone would want."

Beamer wasn't so sure. *Those sentry robots looked old-fashioned in some ways, but outside of science fiction, you couldn't find robots even today as advanced as those were.*

"Actually, I built everything in this room at one time or another," Sol said, waving his hand across the room. "Never came to much, though ... none of it." His voice dripped with regret.

Beamer sipped his drink as he walked along beside one of the covered tables. He thought he could make out a highway and some buildings through the milky plastic drape.

"Go ahead and pull off the plastic," Mr. Parker said to them.

Ghoulie and Beamer put down their drinks. The plastic came off like a wave on the sea, trailing spider silk like drops of spray. They all coughed violently as a cloud of dust billowed in the air.

"Sorry about the dust. I never ... noticed it before," he said through hacking coughs.

What they saw was a sprawling miniature city that looked like downtown Middleton minus the newer buildings. "What is this?" Ghoulie asked.

The old man looked at the scene in puzzlement. "I don't remember," he finally said with a heavy sigh.

Just then Scilla ran over to join them, but she didn't realize how slippery the dust was on the floor and skated into the table. "Oh, I'm so sorry!" she gasped. She didn't hit it all that hard, but a section of buildings was knocked loose.

Suddenly a light blinked on in Sol's eyes. "Pick that up," he said to Ghoulie.

Ghoulie swallowed and carefully removed the buildings. Beneath them was a miniature tunnel snaking its way along beneath the city. Set within the tunnel, one after the other every few inches as if they were ribs for a snake, were rings. About the size of a girl's bracelet in the model, one would have been maybe the height of a house in real life.

Sol wheeled his chair around the table and fingered a switch below. A cylindrical train moved along inside the tunnel rings. The strange thing was it didn't seem to be touching the ground. In fact, it didn't look like it was touching anything—just moving along, suspended in the air amid the row of rings.

"I ... I remember now. This was my ... effort to build a ... a transportation system driven by ... magnetic pulses."

Sol hesitated for a moment, then said, "I wanted to own a railroad. Didn't have enough money, though, so I settled for something smaller—a city trolley company."

"Yeah, we saw the trolley station," Scilla said.

"Oh, it's still there," Solomon asked, "after all these years?"

"It's seen better times," Scilla said with a shrug.

"I'm sure it has. It did well for a number of years. We went ... uh ... bankrupt, though, back in the early nineteen fifties," he said more softly. "That was when the city switched to ... gasoline bus services—no tracks, you see. People were tired of bumping over them in their cars.

"After I lost the trolley company, I dreamed of making new transportation systems," Solomon said as he wheeled over next to Ghoulie. "This is the area of Middleton next to the ... city monument. I built this model ... oh ... fifty years ago, but I couldn't get the city interested. As you can see, it works, but no one believed what their eyes could see. They thought it was all a ... trick," he said with a sound that might have been a grim laugh.

They uncovered more objects in the room. Scilla got the boys to pull off the plastic cover from the big object with claws she had seen when she first entered the room. As it turned out, whatever were at the end of those two arms weren't claws or hands or talons or anything else the three could recognize. But when Sol turned the machine on, a powerful electrical pulse arched between them with a loud sizzle.

"Don't remember what that's for," said Sol. "Everything ... went wrong for ... a very long time." Again he seemed to fade from the present. "I had such dreams," he said with the slightest mocking laugh. "Dreams don't always come true, you know." He coughed and turned back toward the window.

Beamer remembered what Ms. Parker had told them about dreams months ago. She had spoken of all the people on Murphy Street who had gone on to accomplish great things—Nobel Prize winners, writers, musicians, engineers who made spaceships, even great cartoonists. She said she wanted to see if we made our dreams come true. Of course, Beamer's dreams weren't all that big yet. Just getting on first base with a hit was a big enough dream for the moment. But Ms. Parker hadn't said anything about her brother's lost dreams. Had she been wrong? Did some people on Murphy Street see their dreams come crashing down like Sol's?

One thing was for sure: Solomon Parker had given up. That was the only way to explain how he had gotten exiled to this world of cobwebs and discarded projects. Beamer was a little young to understand what it all meant, but it sounded to him like the man had lost *faith*—faith in the fact that, despite all his troubles and disappointments, God would eventually work things out and bless him. That's what his parents had told Beamer to remember when things went wrong. *Okay, maybe a kid's problems weren't in the same league with an adult's, but they always felt like it at the time.*

Solomon suddenly shook his head and swallowed deeply. "I understand you found my train set?" Solomon asked out of nowhere.

"How did you know about that?" Beamer asked, wide-eyed.

"The same way I heard that you were the kids from the tree house," he answered, pointing toward an intercom in the wall. "I overheard you talking to the robot when you came here the first time. I'd forgotten that I even had a train set."

"And it still works," said Ghoulie. "It's amazing, especially when you consider how primitive the technology was at the time."

"Really!" he said with a delighted chuckle. "I'll bet Rebecca has been wondering all these years why her electric bill is so high. I should probably go over to the old house and turn it off."

Suddenly the door opened again, and Mrs. Drummond stalked in with a look of impatience. "I'm sorry to disturb you, Mr. Parker, but it is time for your afternoon nap. These youngsters have taken enough of your time and are probably testing your patience."

"Oh, must they?" the elderly man asked. "It's been so long—"

"We must consider your health, Mr. Parker. I don't want you to become too anxious. Hurry, children!" she said, clapping her hands to speed them up. "Leave your drinks on the table and come along."

"But I never got around to the reason I wanted to see them. I wanted to ask you to take me to your tree house," he said quickly before Mrs. Drummond could usher them out of the room.

Beamer was startled to hear the request, but they were all quick to say, "Yes/Hey, no problem/Sure."

Mrs. Drummond, however, gave him a look of alarm. "The strain would be far too much for you at your age, Mr. Parker. Really, I must insist that—"

"No, no, that's what I want to do," he persisted. "I've waited a long time and, as you suggest, I'm not getting any younger. Please contact me when you think of a good time," he said to Beamer and his friends. "Mrs. Drummond, give them my phone number so that they can call."

"Yes, of course," the stern woman said with a deep frown. "Now we must be going," she said, herding them out of the room like goats. "I knew I should never have admitted you," she muttered after she closed the door. "You'll undermine everything I've tried to do—the very idea of a man in his state of health climbing up to a tree house."

Beamer started to tell her about their transporter/elevator, but she scooted them ahead of her even more quickly toward the staircase. He turned around to look at the others and almost fell down the first couple of steps. He turned forward again and saw Mrs. Drummond at the foot of the steps.

"Come on, don't dally," she said, waving them on down the steps toward her.

How did she get to the bottom of the steps so fast? She looks like Mrs. Drummond, but she can't be. Beamer twisted around to look back up the steps. Mrs. Drummond wasn't up there anymore. *But how could she be the same woman who was just pushing them from behind? There is no way that Mrs. Drummond could have sped past us down the steps to the lower floor without us seeing her.* "Hurry, hurry on out," she said to the kids, holding her hands high as if she were afraid she would get dirty if she touched them.

"Quickly," the woman said as she drove them outside onto the porch. The spiderlike sentries were already there, waiting for instructions. "Make sure to get them off our property and secure the gate behind them."

"But what about the phone number?" Beamer asked as he stumbled backward down the porch steps.

"What phone number?" she asked without a flinch. "Just go away and don't come back!" the now-angry woman said. She whirled around and stalked back into the house.

Beamer stared after her, wondering if she was a witch.

As the woman slammed the door behind her, she saw her twin sister coming down the wide hallway from the back staircase. "My dear Mrs. Drummond, I hope you've done the right thing," she said. "If it had been up to me, I'd have called the police the first time they came, and we would have been done with it."

"—and exposed us to additional public inspection?" Mrs. Drummond shot back at her.

"I hope you are right," said the sister. "Anyway, let's get back to our game. I never realized how much fun Monopoly could be."

"Certainly, Flora, I am anxious to defeat you once again."

12

Meltdown in Never-Never Land

Ghoulie was tossing a bag of marbles in the air when Scilla and Beamer caught up with him in the hallway. There'd been a very early pre-Christmas gift exchange in his homeroom that morning. The guy who gave him the gift snickered that Ghoulie needed new marbles to replace the ones he had lost. What Ghoulie really wanted was the electronic Mars rover building set he had brought. The kid who got it was upset that he would actually have to build it.

The school principal, Mrs. Sopwith, appeared around a corner. "Hello, there," she said with an unusually pleasant smile. "Well, are y'all planning on having a good holiday?" she asked brightly.

"Uh, huh," Beamer said sheepishly. The principal's best friend was Jared's mother. Mrs. Sopwith hadn't given him a friendly look since he'd exposed the bully Jared's little racket with kids and their milk money a few months earlier.

"Well, it certainly looks like we're going to have

a white Christmas, doesn't it?" That was a bit of a stretch since Christmas was still about three weeks off.

"Yes, ma'am," Ghoulie said. Although his tech-talk skills were right up there with Albert Einstein's, he was not very eloquent in the small-talk category.

"Yep," said Scilla, "my grandma's plannin' a big party for our family, and I'm gonna be making the decorations. My cousin is bringin' four kinds of cookies. Uncle Ed is supposed to be in charge of games, but all he really likes to play is horseshoes. As far as I'm concerned—"

"That sounds wonderful, Scilla," the principal interrupted, turning Scilla off as only a teacher could.

One thing Scilla could do very well, though Beamer, *was talk. In fact, finding a way to turn her off would probably make a pretty good science project.*

"Oh, I hope that new friend of yours will have a nice holiday too," she said. Seeing their questioning looks, she went on, "You know, that homeless boy your mother told me about. Are you planning on visiting him any time soon?"

"Well, I don't know ... I suppose," Beamer said with a nervous gulp.

"Do you have any time in mind?" she asked. "I'm sure the sooner you went to him, the better he'd feel. The holidays are especially hard on people who are alone."

"We were thinking maybe next Saturday morning," Scilla chimed in like she was giving a press report.

Beamer gave Scilla a keep-your-mouth-shut look. She shot him back an annoyed grimace.

"Well, that's nice. I'm sure he'll appreciate it," said the principal. "Give my best to your parents," she said as she turned to walk back toward her office.

* * * * *

When the Star-Fighters stepped off the city bus the following Saturday, Beamer scanned the neighborhood like his head was a radar dish. He'd had an uneasy feeling ever since their conversation with the principal. *Still, Jack said he wouldn't show himself until he was sure they were alone.* Beamer saw no sign of any police cars—of any cars at all, for that matter.

It was just the same old deserted, rundown neighborhood—except that the ice Castle/trolley station was melting. Thanks to a gazillion dripping icicles, there were *plop-plop* sounds all around them. Beamer felt like he was tap-dancing all the way to the trolley yard—either that or going crazy from the infamous drip torture.

Beamer, Ghoulie, and Scilla had brought a few presents for Jack—some stuff they'd found cheap on the Internet. "Jack!" Beamer shouted as he approached the sagging snow Castle. Ghoulie and Scilla joined their voices to his, making a little trio singing Jack's name, as if it was a Christmas carol. "Come out, Jack!" Beamer shouted. "It's just us, like we promised."

"If you don't mind," they heard Jack's voice echoing from somewhere, "I'll wait a little longer, just to make sure."

"Well, whatever," Beamer answered, looking for him across the rooftops.

"I hope you guys have done a little practicing with the football since the last time," he said from another direction.

How'd he get over there without anyone seeing him? Beamer wondered. *Maybe he really was Peter Pan. Peter Pan could fly, but he wasn't invisible. Right now, Jack was doing a pretty good job doing the invisible thing.*

They went into the building. The dripping sound was even louder in here as the legions of icicles hanging from the balconies, rafters, and ticket booths shed their frozen weight. The old wooden benches were beginning to peek out through the rolling hills of snow.

"Hey!" Jack yelled again from somewhere above them. "I've been wondering: Who or what is a Star-Fighter?"

The three exchanged glances, rolling their eyes in unison and once more wondering *how they could explain this?*

"Well, you see," Beamer began, looking up toward the voice which now seemed to be above them, "we have this tree house—"

"—and it's shaped like a spaceship," continued Scilla.

"I get it," the invisible boy interrupted. "So, since you play in a pretend spaceship, you call yourselves the Star-Fighters."

Beamer thought he could hear him snicker. "Well, there's a little more to it than that—"

"Hey, I totally understand," said the voice from nowhere. "That's what most kids do—make-believe. Not me, though, I gave that kid stuff up years ago."

"Are you telling me you don't dip into a little fantasy now and then in this 'ice palace' of yours?" asked Ghoulie with a definite smirk. "Come on."

"Well, in case you didn't notice, this ice palace is melting. And besides, ice is cold. I have to spend too much time trying to keep warm and fed to do much playing."

"So why don't you go back to your mom?" Beamer asked. "I'm sure it's plenty warm there with lots of food in the fridge."

"Are you kiddin'? With all the screamin' and carryin' on and the other times when she was totally out of it on drugs? I prefer this reality over that one. Besides, I can't do this there." He suddenly gave an ear-splitting war whoop. "Wahoo!"

They heard a loud bump far above them in the station. Beamer ran out the side door and looked up on the roof. There was Jack, skiing across the rooftop, flying from one roofline to another like he was in the Swiss Alps.

"Yeooooow!" Jack shouted as he sped up one incline and leaped in the air over to another slope of the roof.

His skis didn't look up to snuff for the Winter Olympics.

They were just aluminum slats bent up in front. He vaulted off the roof, flew over their heads, and skidded across the snow on the ground in front of them.

Scilla took a running jump onto a large hub cap and bobsledded over to him. "Come on, Jack. Are you telling us you just abandoned your mom?"

"Hey, y'all have got it backward," Jack answered indignantly. "She abandoned me."

"But you said—" started Beamer.

"Okay, like she didn't kick me out, but she might as well have," Jack interrupted in a huff. He hunched down to remove his skis. "My folks had their own problems. And when those problems got big enough, they forgot I was even in the picture. So, after Dad died and Mom disappeared into druggie land, I couldn't take it any more. I left. The last I heard she moved, so I couldn't find her even if I wanted to."

"But you can't just—/Talk about escaping reality—" Beamer and Scilla said at the same time.

Ghoulie interrupted them. "Hey, did you guys hear that?" he asked, anxiously scanning across the graveyard of trolley cars. "I thought I heard something."

Not hearing Ghoulie, Jack went on. "As far as I'm concerned, a happy family is the most useless fantasy of all. All that huggin' and pattin' only makes you weak when it comes time for a crisis. In the end, people can only rely on themselves."

"But you're still a kid," argued Beamer. "However tough you think you are, there's too much you don't know yet. That's what parents are for—to help you get ready to live on your own!"

"He's right," a woman said brightly as she strode into view around a corner. Several other people were with her, including Beamer's school principal.

At the same time, several policemen suddenly emerged from hiding and circled the kids. "Okay, big shot," one of them said, "we gotcha."

Jack bolted to run, but two policemen quickly blocked his path.

"Let's see, did you say your name was Jack?" the woman in charge asked as she referred to some papers.

Jack looked angrily at the three kids. "So this time you ratted me out for good!"

"No, Jack, we—" stammered Beamer, suddenly feeling a big pit in his stomach.

"You can't count on that being his real name, ma'am," interrupted the commanding policeman.

"Well, for now it's Jack," she responded. "Don't worry, we're not taking you to jail, just to a safe place where you'll have plenty to eat and shelter from the cold."

"I shoulda known better than to trust a bunch of pampered rich kids," Jack spat at the three Star-Fighters.

Beamer looked down, feeling like worm meat. Ghoulie and Scilla also stood a little shamed-faced, avoiding Jack's eyes.

"Jail isn't totally out of the question," said the policeman, correcting the social worker as he took Jack by one arm. "A lot of these homeless kids turn to some pretty heavy-duty theft."

"Not me!" Jack answered angrily. "I've only taken things when I had to, and I always tried to pay it back. I ain't no criminal."

"Take it easy, officer," the social worker said irritably. "You're here only to assist us. We'll take the boy. He's in our charge." She went over and put her arm on Jack's shoulder and starting leading him off. Jack took off toward the station door, but another officer quickly tackled him. They slid together about ten feet, plowing up the wet snow in front of them. When the policeman pulled Jack up, they looked like they should have carrot noses and button eyes.

"I think you'd better let us help you," the policeman said to the social worker with a knowing grimace. "This one's not going to go quietly—or stay quietly either, I'm betting."

The police officers and social worker departed with Jack who kept glaring back at Beamer, Ghoulie, and Scilla until he turned the corner out of sight. The three were left feeling like Benedict Arnold, Judas, and Boba Fett—all in one. The principal ushered the morose trio toward her car.

Beamer wasn't sure why he was so upset. *Jack would definitely be better off with Social Services than alone in the ruins of a station.* Still, when they finally reached the principal's car, Beamer felt the weight of a bowling ball on his chest. From the looks on his friends' faces, he could tell he wasn't the only one.

13

The Lost Star-Fighter

Beamer woke up the next morning with a start.
Something was wrong. He had the feeling he wasn't
alone. His hand itched. He looked down to see a big
black spot in the palm of his hand. It was a pirate's
curse! He was doomed! Then he heard his mother's
voice and woke up again. He shook his head, trying to
clear his thoughts. He looked once more at his hand.
There was nothing there. He gave a big sigh and sunk
back down in his bed. He was definitely taking his guilt
feelings about Jack too far.

He hopped out of bed, went out into the hallway,
and picked up the phone on a small desk. Last night,
his mom had tried to get Jack on the phone, but he'd
hung up when he heard Beamer's name. That had
only made Beamer feel worse. His dad had suggested
they go visit Jack in the Social Services shelter this
evening, where he could explain things to him face-
to-face. So that's what he was going to do.

He dialed the number his mom had used the night before. It proved to be one of the longest calls in the history of mankind. He now knew why his mom had looked so much older by the time she got Jack on the phone the first time. After hearing a recorded message, he was placed on hold for twenty minutes while he listened to Christmas music. Then he was passed around to four departments, where he was placed on hold for twenty more minutes each place. He finally got the shelter. Once more Beamer repeated his request. "What?" he asked with alarm. His face fell and he hung up.

* * * * *

"He's not there," he said later to Scilla and Ghoulie. "He ran away. They told me to tell him, if I saw him, that they had a bed and warm food waiting for him."

The Star-Fighters had been killing time in the tree ship, hoping that they'd take off on an adventure. They didn't care where—to a limburger cheese moon or a planet infested with asparagus—just anyplace where they wouldn't have to think about Jack. But the tree ship hadn't budged.

"Y'all want to go back and check out the trolley station?" Scilla finally asked.

"That's the first place the police would look for him," said Beamer with a heavy sigh. "I think we've lost him."

They were all in "woe is me" position—chin cupped in both hands, arms propped up on elbows—when their second air mail special delivery arrived. A sound like a small fan blowing drew their bleary eyes to a corner window. A miniature hot-air balloon with propellers was gliding toward them on a trail of green smoke. How it could navigate to the tree in the first place—how it missed getting poked, pricked, popped, or radically detoured by all the tree branches—even Ghoulie couldn't imagine. Then it thumped into the tree trunk. *Well, the braking system could use a little work.*

The balloon was shaped like a football, and the gondola looked like a trolley car. That, of course, gave away the source of the message. "It has to be from Sol," Ghoulie exclaimed. A tiny trumpet sounded, and a message popped out of the trumpet. Ghoulie read the message out loud: "Ensign Solomon Parker requests permission to come aboard."

They peered through the branches. "Sol ... uh, Mr. Parker, are you down there?" they yelled on top of each other.

"Hello children!" a familiar breathy, rasping voice called.

"Mr. Parker!" they yelled when they saw a tall, white-haired man leaning on a cane, looking up at them. He was smiling—the first real smile they'd seen on his face.

"Where's your wheelchair?" Scilla called down to him.

"Oh, for some reason, after your visit, I didn't feel like just sitting around any longer. Mrs. Drummond has been giving me fits over the change, so I still sit in it when she's around."

A figure stood next to him wrapped in a white cloak. "Who's your friend?" Ghoulie asked a moment before he glimpsed the gleaming eyes of one of Mr. Parker's spidery robots beneath the white hood.

What do ya know? thought Beamer. *Looks like those long spidery legs can telescope down to man size. Not bad at all for 1940s technology.*

"Don't worry about him," said the old man. "Mrs. Drummond won't let me go anywhere ... alone."

Climbing the tree was definitely beyond Mr. Parker at his age, but Scilla quickly got their transporter/elevator all tuned up and lowered it down to pick him up. Ghoulie rode down to make sure Sol had a safe ride up.

Leaving the bodyguard at the foot of the tree, Ghoulie helped the elderly man into the transporter. He made sure that Sol had a firm grip on the railing and then called up, "Take her up easy."

Scilla hauled them up a lot more smoothly than her usual lurch-bang-lurch, much to Ghoulie's relief, since he didn't know CPR.

"How did you like my little ... uh ... flying messenger?" Mr. Parker asked Ghoulie as they traveled up the tree.

"That was ... uh ... very cool," said Ghoulie, his attention divided between his answer and the slight swing of the transporter in the frigid wind. "How did you control the navigation?"

"Oh, a little sonar mixed in with a little ... programming," the elderly engineer answered. "Primitive by modern standards, I'll grant you. My 'chip' took up the whole gondola."

Beamer was waiting for them at the top as Scilla secured the platform. "Welcome aboard," he said to their friend. "Uh ... I mean ... uh ... permission to come aboard," he added with something close to military precision.

"I told Mrs. Drummond that I was coming here to see my sister and turn off the train set," he said as Scilla helped the old fellow through the door into the tree ship. "That was the only way I could get her to let me out of the house."

"We're sorry," Scilla said. "We would have called you, but Mrs. Drummond wouldn't give us your phone number."

"I suspected something like that might have happened. Funny thing, you'd think she'd be glad that I'm getting back out into the world, but she's not—keeps talking about my heart and high blood pressure and the like."

He coughed and suddenly seemed to teeter backward like a freshly cut tree. All three of them quickly propped him up, giving each other worried looks.

"Well, that was interesting," he said as he took out a handkerchief and wiped a few beads of sweat off his face. "I don't know. Maybe she's right," he said. After a long moment in which their scale of worry went off the chart, he suddenly laughed. "But then, maybe she's not. I'm feeling better than I've felt for forty years," he said, standing up straight and gripping his cane forcefully. "Come on, give me the grand tour."

It was just a tree with a plywood tree house, but Sol looked like he was about to enter Disneyland. They'd been wondering how he'd react to the tree ship. After all, plywood control panels with painted-on dials weren't exactly at the top of the high-tech charts. Of course, that would all change when the ship made one of its "jumps." Actually, they were all hoping that, with such a feeble old man onboard, the ship would stay firmly nestled in the tree branches. Much to their surprise, Sol seemed as happy about the ship in its ramshackle condition as if it were the starship Enterprise. He ran his hands over the ship's hull and the tree branches that held it up as if they were the marble pillars of an ancient temple.

"Oh, I've waited so long to be here," he said, his voice shaking slightly. "You don't know how many years I have resented my sister for depriving me of this adventure. When my trolley company collapsed and I couldn't get a decent position with a railroad, I blamed that failure on my lost opportunity to be one of the Star-Fighters."

Beamer, Scilla, and Ghoulie gave each other a questioning look.

"I know that sounds strange—that a tree house could have such an effect on a person's life, but I'd heard stories about the Star-Fighters—what became of them. Rebecca thought I was just being silly and tried to get it torn down. Billy Stoller's family still owned the property, though, and wouldn't let anyone to touch it." He stood quietly for a moment and then said, "I haven't spoken to Rebecca since ... until today."

He seemed to listen to the creaking of the ship as the tree swayed gently in the wind. "It is, indeed, a magical place. I can feel it. There's more here than I can see." Suddenly Sol laughed. "I'm sure you think me a crazy old man, but I don't care—not anymore," he said as he moved about the ship examining all the gadgets—real and otherwise.

"Well, actually," Beamer said, "most people think we're crazy too."

"I'm not surprised," he said as he looked over the control panels. "You've done some very interesting things here. This monitoring system looks first rate."

"Yep," Ghoulie said proudly. "All the cameras are set up to rotate enough directions so that no part of the yard is hidden."

Sol had some ideas of his own that he shared with them—like how to automate the transporter. He then took out a pad of paper and began figuring out a way to organize the takeoff and landing of multiple spaceships from a single port, until the Star-Fighters reminded him that they only had one spaceship.

"Oh, yes," he said with a chuckle, "I forgot. Spent too many years organizing trolley schedules, I suppose."

He cocked one eye up in puzzlement when he got to the box that was marked Universal Translator. "Uh, does it work?" he asked.

Ghoulie shrugged and said, "If you bang on it now and then." Just for show, he did just that—banged it.

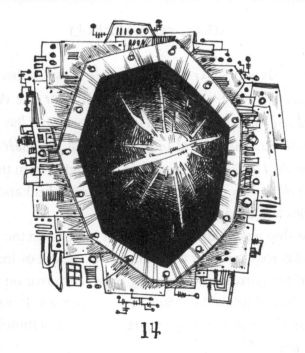

14

Alien Skyjacking

Suddenly the tree ship lurched, and the light outside the windows became streaks of color.

Sol fell back through the cockpit door into the rear compartment, grabbing tables, chairs—anything he could find to slow his fall. But fall he did. He blinked, then rubbed his eyes.

The compartment seemed to be stretching like it was made out of rubber.

Sol blinked his eyes again, as if trying to awaken from one of the weirdest dreams in his life. He felt his stomach tumble and roll. He felt dizzy and told himself to calm down. This hallucination couldn't last long. He swallowed hard and looked out the window.

A star field had replaced the streaks of light. Several large chunks of ice swept past the window.

Maybe I'm having a stroke! Mrs. Drummond was right after all. It had been a mistake to come here. Sol slowly picked himself off the floor and looked around.

One of the ice chunks came very close to the window and was suddenly pulverized in an explosion of white. The ship again lurched and, once more, he began to fall backward. But somehow he spun around and leaped to grab hold of a high ladder.

How did I do that? he thought as he dangled from the ladder. *I'm too old to move like that.* Then he looked at his hands. The wrinkles and the age spots were gone.

The ship jerked again, and he lost his grip on the ladder. He slid across the floor and banged into a wall of lockers. One of the narrow doors sprung open. A mirror on the inside of the door displayed the face of a young man. It was a face he hadn't seen in over sixty years, but it was definitely his. *This is impossible!*

"Secure the ship!" suddenly blared from a hidden speaker. "Secure the ship!" the voice said again.

Is that one of the children? It sounded like the tallest one—Beamer, wasn't it? With the ship still knocking about, Sol pulled himself from locker to locker, to window to wall, panel to table, toward the front of the ship. Finally, he opened a door and stared forward in amazement.

There they were—the three kids—Beamer and ... uh ... Scilla—yes—and Ghoulie—that's right, Ghoulie—such a strange name, Ghoulie. Or was it them? They looked somehow older, like they'd been wearing those uniforms for a long time. Yet this wasn't the tree ship. These kids were manning sections of a very high-tech ship's bridge. "What is happening? Where are we?" he asked.

He saw a viewing screen wrapped around the front of the bridge. It showed a star field with what looked like a large plume of gas straight ahead.

"Stop playing games, Ensign Parker," said the captain who looked like the boy he had known as Beamer. "We haven't identified our exact position yet, but I believe we are somewhere near the Orion Nebula."

"A starship; we're on a starship? But that can't be!" answered Sol.

"Ensign, return to your station," ordered Captain MacIntyre. "We are in the tail of a comet and have no more time for guessing games."

Ensign? He called me Ensign. Sol looked down. Yes, he was in uniform—more white than theirs, but certainly not the same clothes he'd worn when he entered the tree house. *That's right,* he said, remembering. *I was in the tree house—the magical one.*

All of a sudden, his bewilderment ended. As if he'd just made the last twist of a Rubik's Cube, Ensign Parker, a junior officer just out of the academy, suddenly knew who he was and what he had to do. He immediately walked over to the weapons station and began monitoring the sensors.

Again the ship lurched as a spray of ice crystals filled the front screen. Another large ice crystal skittered off the top of the ship.

"Commander Ives!" shouted the captain. "What is that contraption connected to the comet? It looks like some kind of pod swinging on a long cable."

"Well, I may be seeing things," Ives said with a disbelieving grin, "but if I didn't know better, I'd say someone is trying to surf the tail of that comet!"

"Hard to port!" the captain ordered.

Let's see, thought the boy within Commander Ives, *port means … uh, left and—what's right?—oh, yeah, starboard.*

The commander blinked and fired the thrusters that would propel the ship to the left. Even so, an ice chunk sheered off the ship's starboard side and hit the place where the pod's cable was attached to the comet. The pod spun off into space and was caught in the magnetic field of their ship.

"Ensign," Lieutenant Bruzelski called, "see if you can get whatever is riding that pod in through the aft air lock."

"Aye, aye," Ensign Parker said and charged out the door.

Being a Navy man, he knew what *aft* meant. It was funny. In the memory of his Navy days he seemed older than he was now. *How can you be older in a memory?*

Minutes later the ensign was in the very rear of the ship and wearing a space suit. From inside the air lock, he worked one of the ship's robotic arms to pull in the object.

The front of the pod was transparent. The creature inside looked basically human, except that it was covered in fur. It also looked unconscious.

Several minutes later, the door to the bridge opened, and Ensign Parker brought in the creature. Actually, it was the other way around. The alien, holding some kind of weapon, pushed the ensign through the door. The alien could have been a cat, except that it stood upright and had round ears and eyes.

"He panicked when he saw me," said Ensign Parker, "and started screeching and hissing like an alley cat. Believe me, though, he's no kitty cat," he huffed as he massaged his arms. "It was lucky I was wearing that bulky space suit. It took me a half hour to pull him down from the ceiling." Then he shrugged and added, "I didn't see the weapon hidden in his suit until it was too late."

The man who was Sol Parker suddenly rolled back into consciousness. That doesn't sound like me talking. I didn't even talk that way when I was younger. *Maybe it's how I would talk if I were their age right now. But when was now?*

The creature looked at them like they were monsters. Probably thinks he's been abducted by aliens, thought the ensign, which, come to think of it, is exactly what's happened.

The creature began waving his weapon and talking to them in a language with a lot of words that ended with sss.

Captain MacIntyre held out his hands in the universal "calm down" gesture and started using hand signals — the "me Tarzan, you Jane" approach. Lieutenant Bruzelski joined the game, throwing in all kinds of weird gestures and expressions. The alien seemed to calm down when they got his name — Weenoh — out of him.

All at once, Commander Ives slapped himself in the forehead and said, "The universal translator — I forgot all about it." He wheeled his chair over to it and began adjusting the controls. "Keep him talking." A wild combination of hand signals and words continued for awhile until Ives gave them all ear phones and they heard the creature's voice saying, "Dumkoff! Ich liebe an der — "

"German — drat it!" Ives griped. He banged the box.

"Bang Dang," the alien's voice now said in Chinese.

Commander Ives hit the box three more times before they finally heard him say, "%$#$@&^*^*!" A lot of words in English that we can't print.

Attack of the Spider Bots

After some discussion, the Star-Fighters learned that the creature was upset that they had ruined his comet-surfing equipment. He promised that his parents would sue the dickens out of them. It would even be worse, he said, if they didn't take him home immediately. All of this was said along with a lot of hissing and spitting. Ives guessed that he was the equivalent of a teenaged human with a major attitude problem.

"Where is home?" the captain asked him.

"It's that ice-covered moon," Weenoh said, pointing to the lower left corner of the view screen.

"Captain!" said Bruzelski, "Do you see what I'm seeing?"

The Star-Fighters suddenly responded like they'd seen a ghost. The ensign's eyes widened when he saw a space platform dangling just above and to the right of the moon, like a toy hanging from a string.

"Yes, Lieutenant, we're back at the space platform. Change course, Commander Ives, toward that moon," ordered the captain.

"Aye, aye, sir," said the commander.

They continued to toss questions at the young fur ball as the blue-white moon grew in the view screen. Weenoh relaxed and started chatting away. They learned that surfing a comet wasn't unusual for the teenagers of his home. Comets were fairly common in this sector of this solar system. The people had personal force fields that allowed them to bounce off the flying boulders.

As they skimmed down into the moon's atmosphere, alarms began to sound. A shadow suddenly enveloped the ship.

"Ready with those weapons, Ensign?" asked the captain.

"Wait a minute," said Bruzelski. "It's just a white bird."

"A very large bird," echoed Commander Ives. Then another one whisked by.

When a third giant bird joined them, Weenoh's eyes grew into oblong saucers, and his hissing sounds were translated into words like "dead meat" and "crow bait."

"Get us out of here, Commander Ives," the captain ordered. "Battle stations!" he said as an alarm wailed. "Parker, we don't want to shoot unless we have to."

Ives took the ship into a steep corkscrew dive. The birds, however, dived right along with them.

Ghoulie the kid scanned his memory of movie scenes for defensive ideas. *A canyon—that's what I need. I can weave through and make the birds crash into the canyon walls.*

But all he could see were a bunch of icy buttes on the surface, bumping up into the sky like so many frozen smoke stacks. The commander shrugged and began weaving around and through them.

"Oooh," Bruzelski warbled as she began to wobble with dizziness. The captain grabbed a table but still kept weaving around.

Unfortunately, Ives rounded one butte to see a frozen ice shelf hanging between two buttes dead ahead. He sent the ship into another dive to avoid the shelf but ended up plowing into the snowbound turf.

"Aiiiiiiiii" yelled everyone onboard like a heavy-metal band. Weenoh dived for the floor, letting his weapon careen across the room.

One bird crashed into the shelf with an ear-shattering screech, but the other was still coming! Visions of becoming a birdie snack

swirled through the commander's mind as the ship skidded sideways
through the snow. An ice cave suddenly loomed in the path of their
slide. Ives slammed his eyes shut as the ship skimmed between
huge icicles that guarded the entrance like giant teeth.

15

Escape from Ice Planet Zero

At that moment Commander Ives considered the possibility that the cave might not be a cave. He'd seen that in a movie somewhere. In the meantime, though, the remaining bird was trying to reach them through the barrier of ice "teeth." The noise of its squawking was almost as scary as the fact that its claws and beak were getting awfully close. Ives wiped sweat off his brow. How can a guy sweat when he's surrounded by ice?

Suddenly, one of those giant icicles fell, spearing a beak and a claw at the same time. The resulting screech was off the decibel chart! Bruzelski switched off the speakers to rescue their ears. Still squawking bloody murder, the bird flapped its wings, shaking more icicles into falling, and flew away.

"Commander Ives," shouted the captain, "get us out of here before some other life form thinks we're below it on the food chain."

Commander Ives fired the thrusters, and

they shot out of the cave. He shifted the monitor for one last look at the cave. What was that — a tongue licking out after them? Ives shook his head and blinked. It couldn't be, could it?

"Ives, watch where you're going," shouted the lieutenant. The commander switched his view in time to "shoot the gap" between two buttes.

"Keep a wary eye out for those bird things," ordered the captain, "and keep closer to the surface." He picked up Weenoh's weapon. It looked more like a cell phone than a gun. Then he turned to their unwilling visitor. "Weenoh, if you want us to take you home, you'll need to update our guidance system."

Weenoh just shrugged his furry shoulders and pointed ahead and to the right.

"That's what I like — precision," muttered Commander Ives, turning the ship in line with Weenoh's finger.

"Hey, take a look — civilization!" exclaimed Ensign Parker, pointing toward a building that looked like several igloos all patched together. "What is that?" he asked their passenger.

"Fish farm," Weenoh said. "There are many underground lakes where fish have survived the ice age."

"Ice age? Do you mean your home wasn't always an ice world?" asked Bruzelski.

"Of course," Weenoh said, rolling his eyes at what he apparently thought was a stupid question. "Our world was once covered with plants and animals. But that was many thousand eolsss ago."

The translator didn't know what to do with the word eolsss.

Young Ensign Parker suddenly appeared next to the commander.

"Commander Ives, do you realize how many years he's talking about?" he asked in a hushed voice. "My instruments indicate that the planet their moon circles has a very large orbit around its sun."

Ives glanced at the numbers and his eyes grew large. "I wondered how that moon could be so cold next to a super-heated planet and with such a big sun in the sky."

"Me too," said Parker. "That big sun is actually very, very far away!"

"Which means that it's not your everyday red star," the commander added.

"Nope, not even a red giant," said the ensign. "It's a one-in-a-billion red supergiant!"

Giant as in colossal, Ghoulie exclaimed in his head. It was hard enough to visualize a giant star. Those were big enough to swallow earth's sun and the inner planets almost up to earth without so much as a belch. That's a waistline of nearly 300 million miles! But a supergiant could be big enough to swallow the solar system all the way to Jupiter!

"According to my calculations," said the commander as his hands flew over the instrument panel, "one orbit of this planet and its moon takes a little more than a thousand earth years!"

"That's my home straight ahead," Weenoh suddenly interrupted them through the translator box.

Looks of amazement were on every face. Ahead of them was a city. A large palace with towers built upon towers dominated the center. Around it were buildings of every size and shape — all made of ice. There were ice Castles, domed buildings, and ice skyscrapers with soaring spires that pierced the clouds. But they weren't all white like you might expect. Most were multicolored and semi-transparent. Add to these the nearly transparent ribbons that swirled around and through all these buildings and you had a crystal city right out of a fairy tale.

Suddenly, two fireballs streaked by on either side of the ship. The words, "Ichnesss basiness speeleepluss comoraotoss maronuss," blared in their communications system. Two speedy aircraft were on either side of their ship.

Never fails. Somebody always has to get huffy, thought the commander.

"Redirect the signal through the translator," said the captain, and Lieutenant Bruzelski made the adjustments.

"Please identify," said a voice in the speaker. "Passage over the city is restricted."

Captain MacIntyre looked at Weenoh and said, "We are visitors, returning one of your citizens to his home. We mean you no harm. I am turning the communicator over to your citizen who will identify our destination for you."

The captain handed his communicator to Weenoh and nodded for him to speak.

He spoke words they could not understand, but the translator picked up, "I am Weenoh of the house of Sereniusss in sector 5C northwest."

"Safe passage is granted," said the voice through the translator after a moment's pause. "But follow our lead so that we may monitor air traffic for you."

"Nothing like a friendly little escort," said Commander Ives, not really believing there was anything friendly about it. Still his eyes grew large as they flew above freeways crammed with motorized snow sleds and other sleek vehicles.

"It's amazing how you adapted to the change in climate," Ensign Parker said to their visitor.

"Our teachers say that our civilization almost collapsed when waves of panic drove people to riot and revolt."

"I can imagine," said Parker. "How did your people manage to survive?"

"New leaders grew up who drew upon faith that God had not abandoned them and would provide a way," said Weenoh. "I had a test on ancient history two days ago, and I'm pretty sure I aced it. Anyway, driven by that faith, 'people in every profession poured all their resources into adapting their civilization for a colder climate.' That's a quote. I'm sure I got it right. We found new energy sources and improved the older ones. I put in more details about that for extra credit."

"But the lakes and rivers and forests — all the animals — it must have been hard to give them up," said the Lieutenant.

"Yes, we have books and movies and songs and poems about such things. But our forefathers finally accepted the belief that God was leading them to a new dream. We have plenty of wildlife. It's just a different kind of wildlife. We have beautiful buildings. They're just made differently."

"Some scientists want us to repair the space station," said Weenoh. "It is very old — built by the civilization before the ice age. Last eolsss, though, it was voted down because of the cost."

Eolsss can't be the same thing as a year, thought Commander Ives. Maybe it's the time it takes their moon to revolve around the planet.

"I think it would have been really eeeechinoyiass," added the fur ball.

That caused another glitch in the translator. Bruzelski said, "Cool — I think he means it would be really cool ... or maybe hot in their case," she added with a shrug.

There was no open space large enough for the ship to land, but they were able to "beam" Weenoh down into his street.

They'd never tried beaming before, the Ghoulie within the commander suddenly realized. Back in the tree, it was just a plywood elevator lifted by a pulley. But, like everything else, it worked differently during one of their adventures.

Luckily, Weenoh had become much friendlier and no longer threatened that he would get his parents to sue them. Just when everything looked like their trip was going to end up hunky-dory and they were preparing to rocket back to space, a sky full of aircraft blocked their escape. Then they were ordered to follow their air escort and land at the nearest military base.

Well, it's probably what would happen on earth if aliens suddenly dropped in for a little chat, thought the captain. All kinds of diplomats, doctors, and scientists were probably gathering to dissect and study them. Just what they needed — a little vacation in a bubbly test tube. "We appreciate the invitation," he said. "That comet skiing sounds like a lot of fun, but — "

More fire balls crossed their bow. Apparently the inhabitants were running a little short on patience. The next thing the Star-Fighters knew, the speakers were jammed with dozens of voices arguing that the Star-Fighters were really spies for a planet that was planning an invasion. Another shot skid across their bow. Two more grazed their tail. The ship bucked and alarms sounded as Commander Ives fired all thrusters. Then, as it happened, they all blinked.

16

Kidnapped

Once more they were rocking in their plywood tree ship high up in their snow-clad tree. Beamer looked down at Weenoh's weapon in his hand. As Beamer's uniform dissolved back into his everyday clothes, the "weapon" transformed into a snowball and began to melt.

That's when Beamer noticed that alarms were still going off. Or were they? They didn't sound like the ship's alarms.

"Where are the sirens coming from?" asked Scilla.

They heard a groan and turned to see Solomon Parker lying on the floor facedown. He rolled over and opened his eyes. For a moment he just looked puzzled. Then he tried to stand up and groaned again.

"If y'all wouldn't mind, I could use a little help," he said.

All three of them rushed over to help him up. Yep, he was once again old Sol Parker. But even with the groans, his face held a smile bright enough to cause sunburn. "If that was a dream, it's one I never want to forget. If it wasn't a dream then I'm going to have a lot to think about."

The sirens grew louder. Beamer poked his head out the tree-ship door and saw flashing lights over in Murphy Street. "Hey! What's going on?" Seconds later he heard feet crunching quickly through the snow-covered yard below. *What is that—a SWAT team?*

"You, up in the tree," a voice commanded through a bullhorn, "Come down immediately and bring your captive with you."

"Captive?" Scilla asked, her eyes wide.

Beamer could tell that the voice wasn't coming from a patient person. "We'll be right down."

Beamer saw what looked like half the neighborhood on the street as they glided down in their transporter. Paramedics rushed in carrying medical equipment. Beamer's mom and dad were talking with the officer in charge, their faces wearing matching expressions of bewilderment and concern.

"Is there a problem, officer?" Solomon asked as the transporter slowed to a halt.

"Are you Solomon Parker?" the officer asked as he stepped in front of Mr. and Dr. Mac.

"Yes, I am," Solomon responded.

"We received a report that you'd been kidnapped," the officer said as he moved toward the transporter. "All right, you kids, stand clear of Mr. Parker."

"Kidnapped! That's ridiculous!" Solomon said with a huff as the paramedics began checking his vital signs. "I contacted these kids myself and asked them to meet me."

The officer eyed the elderly man suspiciously, then said, "The report also states that you are suffering from Alzheimer's and may be not remember events accurately."

"Mrs. Drummond told you that? I am not aware that I have been diagnosed with that ailment. I'm not even sure what it is."

"Well, that's what it says, and we'll have to investigate the claim." He then turned to the paramedics and asked, "Is he all right?"

One of them removed his stethoscope and looked toward his partner, who said, "His vitals look fine—incredibly good, in fact, considering his age."

"Even so, Mr. Parker," the officer said, "The paramedics will escort you to the hospital where you will receive a full physical."

Solomon protested, "I will go with you peacefully, but please leave the children alone. They have done nothing wrong. In fact, they've just given me one of the best days of my life."

Beamer looked like a boy who was losing a puppy as he watched them lead Sol away. He sighed deeply. *It was like losing Jack all over again. But Sol, at least, could go home.*

*   *   *   *   *

The following Saturday morning came earlier than usual. Beamer was sitting in an ice cream parlor surrounded by seven varieties of shakes and ice cream sundaes. Sitting at the table with him were the mayor, the president, the secretary of defense, and the Joint Chiefs of Staff. They were holding their own shakes, saluting him for once again saving the world from alien invaders. Just as he was bringing one of his shakes to his mouth, Beamer was violently shaken, spilling the drink all over himself. He blinked and saw Ghoulie standing above his bed, shaking him awake.

"What are you doing here?" Beamer asked. Well, actually, his mouth wasn't working quite right yet and he said, "Whaa-oooo-nggggggg-ear."

"Get up!" Ghoulie said in a loud whisper. "I just got a message from Sol."

"A messhhassghh?" Beamer grumbled as he rolled over. "What wassh it—annossherr vallllooooon?" His lips and tongue still weren't in sync.

"No, he's learned how to use a computer," muttered Ghoulie, "but that's not the point. He says he *can't* get out!"

"Whaddya mean he can't get out? It's his house, not a jail. Of course he can get out," Beamer drawled with a yawn. He ducked back under a blanket decorated with jumping rabbits. "How did you get in here, anyway," he mumbled groggily.

"Look, bunny king," Ghoulie said point blank into his ear. "The attic window, how else?"

It dawned on Beamer that Ghoulie had to be pretty serious or he wouldn't have dared to pass ... the web. "Whaddya mean—" Beamer started.

"You already said that," sputtered Ghoulie. "She's locked him up."

"Who has?" asked Beamer bolting up in bed.

"Mrs. Drummond has, of course! Man, I hope you never have to determine the fate of the world before nine o'clock in the morning."

Beamer finally rolled out of bed, literally, hitting the floor with an impressive thump.

* * * * *

About an hour later the kids arrived at the gate of Solomon's house. Beamer pushed the call button. Once again Mrs. Drummond's recorded voice answered, "We are not receiving unsolicited visitors at this time. However, if you have a visitor's pass—"

Kidnapped

"This is Beamer MacIntyre with the Star-Fighters," Beamer interrupted. "We believe that Mr. Parker would like to see us."

The previous message started to repeat but was interrupted when Mrs. Drummond's face popped up on the video screen. "I'm afraid you are mistaken, children," she said stiffly while hurriedly attaching a hat. It was a tall hat, roughly resembling the top half of a rooster—comb, tail, and all. "Mr. Parker has no desire whatsoever to see you after the trouble you caused him."

"It was not *us* who caused him trouble," Scilla jumped in to say.

Ghoulie joined in, "We already know he wants to see us! He sent us a message. Put him on the screen … please!" he added.

"I most certainly will not!" Mrs. Drummond responded in a huff. "For that matter, he is not here. He is in the hospital!"

The kids gasped, depriving several nearby insects of their air supply.

Mrs. Drummond's voice became harder. "You are to make no further attempts to see him. Do you understand? He is no longer competent to manage his affairs. I am petitioning the court later this afternoon for permission to make all his decisions for him in the future. And rest assured that I will alert the authorities if you try to contact him again."

The screen went blank, but they felt like a door had just been slammed in their faces.

"No," Scilla cried with a pained look, "he was just beginning to come back to life! Please tell me she can't do this!"

"I don't know," Ghoulie said with a lump in his throat. "I'll ask my mom."

They heard a car start up. Moments later, the engine grew

115

louder as the car approached.

"Get out of sight!" Beamer said, pushing them away from the gate. They ran back and huddled against the wall.

The gate opened, and they watched the limousine pull into the street. "Look at the window, y'all," said Scilla as the car drove away from them.

"Yes, I saw her," said Beamer glumly.

"No, the back window," Scilla said with a jab to his shoulder. "There are two of them." Two identical heads appeared side by side in the back window—rooster tail hats bouncing up and down in unison.

17

Tunnels in the Sky

In spite of Beamer's protests about the urgency of saving Mr. Parker, his parents had insisted that they would look into it on Monday. In the meantime, he would have to finish his usual Saturday chores. So it was several hours later, after he'd swept out the basement and cleaned off the front porch, before the three Star-Fighters were all able to gather up in the tree ship. "We can't let Mrs. Drummond take over Solomon's life," said Beamer between clenched teeth

"You mean Mrs. Drummond and her twin," Scilla said, correcting him.

"Okay, she or they are using his trip to our tree ship as an excuse. Just because an old man has fun doesn't mean that he's losing his mind."

"In case you haven't noticed," said Ghoulie, "we are just kids. There's not a whole lot we can do."

"No, we're missing something here," said Beamer. "Those twins know as well as we that he's not out of his mind. They're up to something—"

"So we gotta find out what," Scilla finished for him with her face scrunched thoughtfully.

"How are we going to do that?" Ghoulie asked in frustration. "I doubt if it's on the Internet."

"What we gotta do is get back into that house before the two old ladies get back," said Beamer as he paced around.

Just then a thump sounded above their heads.

"Now what?" groaned Beamer, "an invasion by Bigfoot?"

Suddenly a face appeared upside down in the cockpit window. They jumped as if they'd seen a ghost. Beamer's first impulse was to make a run for it. After all, the last time they saw Jack, he looked like a shark hungry for three guppies.

But then Beamer noticed something: the tree in which the ship was cradled was perfectly quiet. The last time somebody came up the tree determined to hurt somebody, a whirlwind grew up around the tree, and a huge cloud of insects chased the invaders away. The tree didn't like people with "malice in their hearts," as Old Lady Parker had put it. Of course, since it was winter, there weren't many insects around, but the tree probably had other weapons. Then Beamer saw Jack's face crease into a smile.

"Hey, Star-Fighters," he yelled from outside the window, "Got room for a visitor?"

They all cheered and rushed outside to bring him in.

"Where have you been?" Scilla asked. "Beamer called the shelter, and they said you'd run away."

"Yeah, well, that place was okay," Jack said with a shrug, "and I know them folks were only tryin' to help out, but it wasn't for me. No, sir, it was way too limitin'. I felt like I was in prison, whether they meant it that way or not. I had to get outta there. But if you think I'm gonna tell you where I am now ..." he said with a grin at Scilla. "Not a chance."

"We didn't think you'd ever want to see us again," said Beamer with a wary look.

"Yeah, I thought y'all were a lower form of life for awhile, but then I learned that ya didn't know y'all were being set up."

"How did you find us?" asked Ghoulie. "We never told you where we lived."

"Hey, just because I live on the streets doesn't mean I'm technologically challenged. I know all about phone books. And scanning a few blocks of sidewalks, curbs, and drains can give you enough change for bus fare."

"Beamer," Scilla whispered to him, "we've gotta talk to him about his mama. He can't—"

"Not now," Beamer whispered back to her.

Jack finally began taking in his surroundings. "So this is your famous spaceship in a tree, huh? You say you can make warp speed in this box," Jack said as he strolled into the cockpit. "Nice paint job," he added as he touched the painted dials. "Looks to me like your brains do most of the warping—no offense, of course," he added quickly before their faces could change color too much. "You folks definitely have healthy imaginations. I'm just wondering if yours is a little too healthy," he said with a laugh.

Scilla nudged Beamer, but Beamer already had an idea popping into his head. "Hey, we've gotta little problem. You just might be the guy who can help us fix it." Scilla and Ghoulie gave Beamer a questioning look.

"Well, I'll check my corporate calendar," Jack answered cheerfully, "but I suspect I can move a couple of appointments around."

*   *   *   *   *

The block which enclosed Solomon Parker's house was much bigger than Ghoulie had thought. It was already getting dark, and he was going to have to get home pretty soon for dinner. "What are you looking for?" he shouted to Jack, who had already led them almost halfway around the block. "I don't think you're going to find an open gate or a secret passage, if that's what you're looking for."

"You'd be surprised," Jack whispered loudly over his shoulder.

"What's that supposed to mean?" Ghoulie called to Scilla, who was directly in front of him. "I hate it when people put hidden meanings into their words."

"Shhh!" Scilla hissed back at him. "Keep your voice down. We're supposed to be sneaking into this place, not broadcasting our arrival to the world."

"Okay, okay," Ghoulie whispered in a huff. "I just don't see how we can sneak into this place without invisibility cloaks and antigravity pods, and they haven't been invented yet." *Why doesn't anybody ever listen to me?* He'd already considered the possibilities and there was just no way! "You guys haven't forgotten about those robots, have you?"

"Look, Ghoulie," Beamer said impatiently, "The two Mrs. Drummonds are out of the house right now. We may never have another chance to find out what they're up to. And when it comes to finding hidden spaces and getting around obstacles, Jack's an expert."

"All right," Jack said as he suddenly pulled to a stop—too suddenly as Scilla back-ended him, and Ghoulie back-ended her, making Jack lurch forward another step "Will y'all quit the Keystone Cops thing," Jack said as he straightened his hat. "I think I see a way." He jogged across the street and then took off down a sidewalk.

"Hey!" Ghoulie shouted. "You are going the wrong way!" *Clearly the guy's brain cells were iced over from too many nights in the cold air.* "The house is back—"

"Ghoulie—hush!" Scilla hissed at him.

"Trust him, Ghoulie," Beamer said as he started chasing Jack.

About half a block later, Jack stopped beneath a cluster of trees. Jack launched himself up one of the smaller trees. "Come on," he shouted down to them. "You guys ought to be experts at climbing trees by now."

"Yeah," groaned Ghoulie, "but there's no tree house up this one, and it's a block away from Mr. Parker's house. I don't need any exercise. I get enough P.E. in school."

"Move it, Ghoulie," Beamer said.

Jack cut up through a smaller tree until he could hop over to one of the lower branches on the big elm tree. That's what most of the trees were around here—elm trees. "Okay, so there'd better be a point to all this," Ghoulie grumbled as he joined the others beside Jack.

"This is something I discovered on the way over to your tree ship," Jack said. "I'd seen some cop cars about a block from your place and hid in a tree. Check it out," he said as he pointed along a line of trees

Ghoulie reluctantly followed Jack's finger. After he uncrossed his eyes, he saw a seemingly endless stretch of entwining branches. "So," he said with a smirk, "the neighborhood has a lot of trees."

"Very big and very old trees," echoed Scilla, her eyes squinting as if she were trying to decipher an ink-blot picture.

Beamer had almost the same expression on his face. Then his eyes widened. "There's a tunnel!" he said in astonishment.

18

Lost Treasure

"A what?" Ghoulie asked as he tilted his head for another look.

"Yep," Jack said as proudly as if he were Indiana Jones finding a hidden door to an ancient temple. "You have passages through your trees."

Now even Ghoulie's eyes grew wide. "Whoa! You're right." The tree branches formed an arch around an open space in which there were practically no branches. The branches below were thicker than usual, making it easier to step from branch to branch while holding on to the branches above. "How could that happen? I mean, who—"

"Or what," added Scilla, "would have made a passage through trees?"

"Good question," said Jack. "These trees are probably a couple hundred years old. It could have been made any time."

"Yeah," said Ghoulie, "but it had to have been continually used over the years or the branches would have filled in."

The passage through the trees wove around, turning one way or another or going up and down, but never so extreme that they couldn't keep going. Once in awhile, another passage intersected theirs, winding away to who knew where. Finally Jack stopped. Mr. Parker's house lay across the street. The path through the trees continued across his yard all the way to the house.

A few minutes later, they quietly dropped from a tree branch onto the roof, not far from a row of attic windows.

"What if the windows are locked?" asked Ghoulie, on a roll in the complaint department.

That's what getting up early on Saturday morning does to you, thought Beamer. "It's possible," he said, "but most people don't bother to lock attic windows. We don't."

He was wrong. Mrs. Drummond was definitely not "most people." The rooftop SWAT team went from window to window, looking in vain for one she or her robot crew had overlooked. What was worse, Ghoulie was finding all sorts of ways to say "I told you so."

Luckily, or perhaps thanks to a nudge from a passing angel, Jack took a shortcut across the ridge of the roof and knocked loose an old vent. They climbed in. It was a tight squeeze. Taking a breath was not an option unless you wanted to become a permanent fixture in the ventilation system. Once Jack was through the opening, he was able to haul himself down a beam in the steep-angled ceiling to the floor. Then he stacked up boxes like toy blocks for the others to climb down.

The attic was loaded with toys or robots—it was hard to tell which—in every size and shape. Since most of them had missing pieces—heads, arms, feet, rollers, eyes, etc., Beamer figured these were Sol's rejects.

It might have made a great playground if it weren't for the fact that the whole menagerie was wrapped together in about fourteen layers of cobwebs. The rocketeering gang hadn't gone more than thirty feet before they'd destroyed half a dozen spider civilizations.

Yep, no question about it—sooner or later those little buggers were going to take over the world. For that matter, the web in his attic might be the headquarters for a spider invasion fleet! Beamer grabbed a robotic arm and began using it like a machete to clear away a path through the webs.

All of a sudden, the silence was broken by a voice that rumbled like a truck engine: "State your name and purpose!" They whirled around and were suddenly blinded by a light.

There was only one thing to do: panic! Like rats scurrying from a fire, they scattered about the attic.

"Surrender or I will be forced to subdue you." It was a broken-down robot! The machine careened about pursuing them. "You cannot escape." With every few words, the machine's deep voice suddenly screeched in a high pitch like the voice of a boy going through puberty. The chase wound all over the attic—up, over, down, and around all the junk and the sticky webs. Before they knew it, they'd been herded like cattle into a corner of the attic. Then the robot shot a gun: a net flew out. They tried to dive out of the way, but the net covered them like a fresh catch of flopping tuna. *Okay,* Beamer thought, *so they were tuna cattle, except that, by now, they were all almost totally wound up in gummy spider silk. Well, one thing was clear—from mammal to fish to insect—they were definitely working their way down the food chain!*

"It's a robot," he whispered loudly, "with a light on its head like a coal miner—probably an earlier version of Solomon's sentry robots."

So much for rescuing Mr. Parker! Who was going to rescue them? Assuming they would live long enough to be rescued, that is. For one thing, Beamer had forgotten to tell anyone where they were going. Of course, if he had told them, they'd have never let him go on this cockamamie expedition. For another, the robot was tightening the net—very tightly. Beamer might have to give up breathing again. Just when his ankle was about to become connected to Scilla's chin, a shadow appeared in front of the robot's light beam and Beamer heard a click.

"I always say, when in doubt, try the on/off switch."

That was Jack's voice. Beamer figured that he had managed to dive out of the way as the rest of them were being penned in and circled around behind the robot.

"Get your toe out of my nose," Beamer grumbled at Scilla as he slowly unwound his elbows and knees. "Why are you wearing toeless shoes in the middle of December, anyway?"

"Hey, there's nothin' wrong with my toes," Scilla shot back at him.

"Now we've gotta find our way to Mrs. Drummond's office," Ghoulie said.

"Who said she had an office?" asked Beamer.

"If she pays the bills and manages the household, like Sol said," answered Ghoulie, "she's bound to have some place where she keeps all her household records. And that's where we'll probably find whatever we're looking for."

"Yeah, I think I saw it when we were here before," Scilla said thoughtfully. "She'd left the door open."

"Well, then lead on," Beamer said to her with a sweep of his hand, like a knight addressing a queen, "but we've gotta hurry. Those twins could come back at any time." Beamer was surprised they weren't home already, but he'd noticed the limousine was not where it was usually parked when he'd checked from the rooftop. He figured they must have gone to a movie or something.

"Yeah ... right," Scilla said sarcastically. "And I could probably find it if we'd come in the front door. But from the attic?—haven't got a clue."

One of those neat pictorial maps like you see in malls would have come in handy—you know, the ones that say, "You are here," with a map showing where everything else was. They found their way out of the attic and began winding through the hallways.

It would also have been nice if there hadn't been video cameras and infrared sensing devices in every corner. You'd have thought they were in the Smithsonian. Jack came to the rescue again. He brought out an aerosol can and sprayed the camera lenses. He also used it to reveal those red beams from the infrared sensors. Beamer had wondered why Jack had so many pockets. *Maybe street people thought they had to be ready for every situation.* Eventually they found a hallway that they remembered from before. Scilla took the lead and, after only five wrong turns, finally found Mrs. Drummond's office door down on the first floor.

Unfortunately, the door was locked—no surprise there, of course. Beamer wondered if Jack was going to pull out a skeleton key, but he didn't. He did try to pick the lock, but his breaking-and-entering skills weren't quite up to it.

Scilla suddenly had to go to the bathroom. Actually, she'd been wiggling like a jellyfish for the past ten minutes, which was probably why she'd made so many wrong turns. She tried the room next door and, to her relief, found it to be the bathroom. Meanwhile, Jack returned to trying to pick the lock while Beamer worked on the hinges.

A couple minutes later, Scilla opened the bathroom door and leaned against it with a satisfied grin. "Guess what?" she said. "There's a door from her office into the bathroom ... and guess what?"

"Enough with the guesses," grumbled Ghoulie.

"It's unlocked!"

Mrs. Drummond's office was small compared to other rooms they'd seen in this house, but it was still bigger than any two rooms in Beamer's house. However, Mrs. Drummond was strictly low tech. Nothing resembling a computer, fax machine, copier, or printer was in sight. Both her typewriter and her phone were clearly BPC (Before Personal Computing). Beamer wondered if the electricity was also antique, but the lights worked. Of course, that might have been because the lamps were also antique. Anyway, there was enough light for them to do the grunt work of searching through the filing cabinets and the boxes of records stacked in the large closet. At least there were no cobwebs to worry about—just paper, lots of paper.

Eventually, Scilla's bird-like voice echoed from the closet. "Hey y'all, I think I found somethin'." They found her sitting spread-eagled on the closet floor almost buried in large envelopes. "I don't know what they are, but they have a lot of big numbers on them," she said as she handed an envelope up to Ghoulie.

Ghoulie flipped through the pages and said, "Stock certificates—these are stock certificates!"

"What's that?" Jack asked.

"Well, here's the name of a railroad company," Ghoulie said, pointing to the heading. "And this number tells how much stock he has in the company—"

"What's stock?" asked Scilla.

"I'm not sure, except that my dad has lots of them," said Ghoulie. "It has something to do with how many pieces of a company you own."

"How do you own a *piece* of a company?" asked Jack.

"I think I get it," chimed in Beamer. "It's like if we all chipped in to buy a box of firecrackers. We'd each own part of the box load, assuming we all put in the same amount of money, that is."

"I think these numbers say how much Mr. Parker's stock is worth," said Ghoulie, his face all scrunched up figuring.

"Wait a minute," Beamer said, pointing to the upper right hand of the page, "This says 1962. That's prehistoric!

"You're right," Ghoulie said with a shrug. "For all we know, he could have sold them all off by now. Do any of those envelopes have a more recent date?" he asked Scilla.

She rummaged through them quickly and finally said, "Sorry." Getting ready to stand up, she plopped the stack of envelopes on the floor creating a cloud of dust that made them all sneeze.

"Then look around," Ghoulie said, "and see if you can find more of these—some with less dust on them."

They scattered, looking for anything that had to do with stock, or a railroad company, or money in general. Beamer finally made his way to Mrs. Drummond's desk. He opened one drawer, then another, and then spotted something on top of the desk. Things on the desk were very neatly arranged. But just edging out the side of a folder was a piece of paper with the name of the railroad. He opened the folder and stared. "Hey guys, I got it!"

The others crowded around him, staring at the report. Scilla started counting the number of zeroes then the number of numbers before the zeroes. Ghoulie snatched it from her hand. "Hey!" she protested.

"Uh ... guys," Ghoulie said as he took a deep gulp. "This is way beyond millions!"

"And look at this!" Scilla said, holding up a ledger they had knocked onto the floor when they were scrambling for the stock report. She flipped it open to where her thumb was holding a place. "It's the household budget, but it doesn't look anything like my grandma's budget."

"Beamer's eyes grew even bigger. "Since when does anyone need $50,000 for a month's worth of groceries?"

"So that's it then," Scilla said in hushed amazement.

"She—or they—want his millions!"

"Sure looks that way," said Beamer. "Come on, let's get out of here."

Suddenly they heard a key in the lock. Ghoulie hurriedly tucked the report back into the folder as the door opened.

19

Triple Trouble

"I told my sisters they should have called the police on you the first time!"

"Holy tamole! There are three of them!" Scilla said with a gasp.

It was another Mrs. Drummond! This Mrs. Drummond, though, walked with a cane.

"Triplets!" Beamer echoed her. "Run for it!" he cried as he ran for the bathroom door. Before Mrs. Drummond the third could figure out what they were doing, they were through the bathroom and into the hallway behind her.

"Stop, you children, or I'll call the police!" she cried out.

"No you won't," Beamer yelled back at her, "unless you want the police to see what you've been doing with Mr. Parker's money."

She pulled up short with a look of uncertainty. Then she clenched her jaw and went to the nearest wall communicator. "Security! Security!" she said into the wall, "Intruder alert! Close down all exits. Apprehend four children now in the main hallway."

"Hurry!" cried Beamer. Abandoning any attempt at secrecy, they galloped up the steps like a herd of goats. In the background, Beamer heard mechanical voices on communicators relaying orders for intercepting them in this hallway or that one. More alarms went off as they rushed past cameras and sensors they didn't bother to mask. Finally they reached the attic. They saw lights sweeping the grounds outside the windows. Not wanting to squeeze back through the vent, Beamer unlocked one of the attic windows and removed the screen. They poured out onto the roof to find lights sweeping up there too.

"Watch out!" cried Beamer as a searchlight swept toward them. Scilla and Ghoulie ducked behind a chimney while Jack and Beamer slid to the other side of the roof, hanging on to the ridgeline for dear life.

That's the way things went for awhile—ducking between roof lines and behind chimneys—until they reached the big tree. Not surprisingly, the house security system did not expect intruders to be exiting along a passage through the trees. Few lights swept the trees.

Did Solomon Parker know that a "treeway" led to his house? Why would anyone make all these passages? Did they go up to every house or just some of them and why? How many mysteries could one street have?

When they finally made it to the tree across the street, they gave a collective sigh big enough to bring snow down on their heads. They stood there at the intersection of several branches, gasping for air and looking like ice cream sundaes.

* * * * *

Beamer showed his dad the folder they had found, while Ghoulie and Scilla looked on in hushed excitement. Jack had already headed back to wherever he was living, afraid that Beamer's mom would turn him back in to Social Services. As Beamer expected, he had to take a pretty good tongue-lashing, not only for being late to dinner but for breaking into someone's house.

"But—" Beamer started to say several times. He wondered what it would be like being grounded until he was thirty.

"No, get it into your head," Mr. MacIntyre said with his finger about to poke a hole in Beamer's sinuses. "Something like this could put you in juvenile hall!" Finally his father's eyes turned back to the paper. "But I see your point. We'll have to get this to a lawyer right away."

"What about Ghoulie's mom?" Beamer asked, still breathless with excitement. "She's a lawyer."

"Yes," said Ghoulie, "a pretty good one too."

"We can begin with her, anyway," said Beamer's mom. "Now if you all wouldn't mind, it's time for Beamer to go to bed ... without his dinner." Beamer groaned and headed for the stairs while the other kids made a swift exit.

* * * * *

And so the legal machine started to grind, as Beamer's dad put it. Exactly how a machine with no gears and bolts or other metal parts ground anything, Beamer had no idea.

The full story came out piece by piece. Just as Beamer expected, Solomon's shares in the railroad had grown until, for all practical purposes, he owned a railroad company. But since he had never answered mail or messages or telegrams from the company, the railroad had gone on without him.

Mrs. Drummond had kept the truth from him while collecting the share in the profits the company regularly sent to Mr. Parker. Right away, Mrs. Drummond accused the Star-Fighters of breaking and entering. Nobody made them go to jail just yet, but there was the possibility that, if she won her case, they just might. Wearing an orange jumpsuit and hammering rocks the rest of his life didn't sound like a great career move to Beamer.

Mrs. Drummond had most of Solomon's money firmly in her hands and could afford to pay bogus doctors to declare that he was wacky and high-priced lawyers to help her handle the stocks. Things were looking bad for both Solomon Parker and the Star-Fighters.

Then Old Lady Parker got wind of what was happening to her brother. She had little love for Solomon but tremendous loyalty for the family name. She wasn't going to let anyone swindle a Parker. Like a force of nature, she blew into the halls of justice and got a judge to freeze her brother's accounts. That meant Mrs. Drummond could no longer use his money. Finally, with Mrs. Drummond's high-priced lawyers no longer blocking the way, evidence began stacking up against her and her sisters.

Yep, all of Mrs. Drummond's claims about Mr. Parker's sanity and about her right to control his money were finally overturned. At the same time, her breaking and entering charges against the Star-Fighters were also dismissed, and Beamer no longer had to worry about how he would look wearing a bright orange suit.

On the day they heard the news, Scilla started singing "Ding, Dong, the Witch is Dead" until the boys and, eventually, Beamer's mom and dad joined in. It was like having Christmas before Christmas, except that the good news was the only present. They drank hot cider and eggnog and munched on Dr. Mac's Christmas cookies until way past bedtime. It was too bad Jack couldn't be with them, but he wasn't about to drop in where adults were hanging around. He'd visited the tree ship a couple times since the break-in, and each time they'd told him the latest about the Parker case, but they had no way of contacting him on their own.

Then, like a dragon stripped of her treasure hoard and with only one fiery breath left, Mrs. Drummond hurled her last fireball! She had the tree ship condemned!

The Star-Fighters never saw it coming. When the news arrived two days after their little celebration, Beamer felt like he'd been hit by a nuclear shock wave. When he called to tell Ghoulie and Scilla the bad news, they had the same reaction. They were all tongue-tied, unable to speak.

"Can she really do that?" Scilla asked as she crab-walked up a large tree branch toward the tree ship later that day.

"Apparently so," Beamer said gloomily. "Dad called up the officials right away and argued with them about it. 'It's just a kids' tree house,' they said. Dad told them how he and Mom had reinforced the tree house to make it safe, but they said safety wasn't the problem. It was just higher in the tree than city building regulations allowed and had to be torn down."

"Maybe we could take it apart and put it back together lower down in the tree," Ghoulie said with a hopeful shrug as he came out of the tree ship.

"It won't fit anyplace lower," Scilla said, shaking her head.

"How do you know that?" Beamer grumbled to her.

"Hey, I know this tree better than anybody," Scilla said with a smug look. "I'd been playing in this tree long before Beamer even moved into the neighborhood. Besides," she went on in a more mysterious tone, "what would happen to the ... oh, you know what I mean ... if we tried to move or rebuild the tree ship?"

"Oh, I never even thought about that," Beamer said, his eyes widening.

"What are you guys talking about?" Ghoulie snapped impatiently. Then it struck him, and his eyes got bigger too. "You mean our little ... jumps into other worlds," he said, not really knowing what to call it.

"Yeah," Beamer muttered with a heavy sigh, "that little touch of the miraculous we haven't figured out yet."

Beamer didn't know it, but at that very moment his mother was at City Hall, trying another ploy. She figured that since the tree ship was pretty old and practically a legend in the community, she might get the city to declare the tree house a "historical monument." It was a shot in the dark and, unfortunately, it didn't work. She did manage to give the people there a good laugh. It wasn't exactly the Christmas cheer she had in mind.

"Well, it was worth a try," she said with a shrug that night at dinner. Beamer's father smiled, got up from his chair, and came over behind her and wrapped her up in a big bear hug. It was all way too mushy for Beamer.

As he went back to his dinner chair, Beamer's dad said, "I've decided I just can't do it. If the city wants the tree house down, they are going to have to do it themselves. I imagine we'll have to pay for it, but—"

Beamer couldn't tell if his dad was choked up or not, but he didn't finish his sentence. For some reason, though, what he said gave Beamer a strange feeling, like a warm glow, inside. Then when his dad prayed over dinner, he asked that God would work things out for the best. *Sometimes being part of a family that trusts in God is a pretty neat thing.*

The next morning, Ghoulie's mother called Beamer's mom and dad from the courthouse. In a last ditch effort, Old Lady Parker herself had approached the mayor personally to convince him to grant an "exception" to the height rule. Word was that she had known the mayor since he was "knee-high to a chipmunk" and if he couldn't bend the rules for the sake of her neighbor's tree house, then he couldn't expect any more election donations from the Parker family.

Everyone breathed a sigh of relief. It was going to be a great Christmas after all. There was no way the mayor could ignore Ms. Parker's request. Nobody ever ignored Ms. Parker.

Two days later, Beamer's Xbox time was interrupted by the rattle and groan of old trucks in the street. He and Ghoulie ran to the window and saw the approach of doom. Several men jumped off the back of a flatbed truck as another truck pulled up with a machine for grinding up tree limbs.

"What's happening?" Beamer cried as he ran out the front door.

"Just following orders," the man in charge said as they pulled out their axes, chain saws, and other equipment.

Ghoulie ran alongside the grinding machine as it backed up the driveway toward the tree in the backyard. "Hey, you can't do this. The mayor said—"

"The mayor changed his mind," the man interrupted him as he pushed the boys out of the way. Only much later did Beamer learn what had happened. The mayor discovered that Ms. Parker had failed to contribute anything to his last two election funds. The destruction of the tree house became the mayor's personal payback to Ms. Parker.

Scilla saw what was happening from her second-story bedroom and ran down to throw in a few complaints of her own. "That's our tree!" she yelled. "You can't just bust in and—"

Somebody revved up his chain saw, and Scilla's cries could no longer be heard.

Phones all over the neighborhood began ringing and, by the time the workmen had assembled their equipment, the Star-Fighters and all their assorted parents, guardians, nannies, and siblings were under the tree. The half of the neighborhood that had been there when the police came the first time was back. Some of them even carried placards protesting the tearing down of the tree house. A few of them shouted at the workmen—things they shouldn't have said, especially since it wasn't the workers' fault.

As the workmen approached the tree, a hush fell over the crowd. It parted to allow a powerfully large, elderly woman dressed in black to pass through. It was Old Lady Parker looking like a thundercloud on the verge of shedding lightning. Beamer hadn't thought it was possible, but it looked like she had even more and deeper wrinkles than she'd had the first time they saw her. And she looked just as scary.

Seeing her expression, the unpopular crew hurried to the tree. Beamer's little brother, Michael, started throwing acorns at them until his mother made him empty his hands and pockets. Beamer appreciated the support. He expected his sister, Erin, to pass out gifts to the demolition crew. Amazingly, she kept wiping tears out of her eyes. As far as he knew, her only contact with the tree had come when she threw things out her window to get the ship's crew to quiet down. *Girls were definitely strange creatures.*

Ms. Parker spat out a vow to pour millions into supporting the mayor's next opponent. Then, with the grace of a mountain rotating on a pin, she turned, retreated through the crowd, and disappeared. Eyes were wet with tears, and the sound of sniffles filled the air. The workmen swallowed as if they had received a terrible curse, but they resumed their course up the tree. Beamer had never felt so helpless. At least against Jared, he'd been able to put up a fight. Now, there was nothing left to do. The tree ship was lost!

20

The Return

Then something happened. Beamer should have known it would. Yep, the tree, or the energy field around the tree, went into self-defense mode. Slowly the wind began to rise. Beamer almost didn't notice it at first. Before long, though, the wind turned into a whirlwind. It spun around and through the tree, picking up what was left of the snow. Soon the workers found themselves in a full-scale blizzard.

The branches also flailed about in the wind, whipping the men like a thousand switches. It wasn't hard enough to really hurt them but enough to—you know—*hurt, like a spanking*. The men began yelling at each other and the tree, holding onto the tree for dear life while everything they were carrying was ripped away by the wind and flung down into the safety net Beamer's mom had strung out below the tree.

Beamer's mom and dad remembered all the wild and crazy things their son had said about the tree and the tree ship and gave Beamer a puzzled look. The protestors couldn't tell what was going on. They just thought the workmen were tearing the tree house to smithereens.

Pretty soon the blizzard in the tree became so strong that several workmen began to lose their footing and fall into the net. People in the crowd stepped forward to help them out of the net. As it turned out, none of the workmen had so much as a scratch, but all of them had felt seconds away from seeing that bright tunnel of light in the sky.

"How come the storm's only in the tree?" one of the workmen asked after he crawled out of the net, totally bewildered at how still the air was away from the tree.

"There's no way I'm going back into the tree!" one of the workmen said to his boss. "That thing is haunted!" he said, pointing up toward the tree ship.

"Yeah!/He's right/Me neither" the other men shouted in agreement, though none of them apparently felt comfortable using the word "haunted."

The leader took off his hard hat and scratched his head, trying to think through their predicament. "Yeah, you're right," he finally admitted, shaking his head, "I think we have … some … uh, natural …. obstacles which make it impossible to complete this job. I'll figure out how to word it in the report later," he said, waving his hands in the air, "Come on, boys, let's pack up and get out of here."

They never came back.

* * * * *

Beamer would never forget the day Solomon came home from the hospital. It was only a few days before Christmas. A huge stack of luggage made a small mountain in the entry hall. Mrs. Drummond and her sisters stood nearby as prim and snobbish as always while they waited for Mr. Solomon's car. Between sniffles and blowing noses, they glanced fearfully up at the large figure standing like a monument at the top of the staircase. Old Lady Parker's voice boomed orders while her hands cut the air like she was wielding a wizard's staff. An army of servants did her bidding, moving up and down the stairs and back and forth from room to room. Meanwhile her searing gaze always returned to the triplets. If eyes could shoot lightning, those ladies would have been roast geese.

Solomon's cane gently tapped the floor as he walked over to his former assistant and her sisters. Scilla wondered what was going through his head. His face looked hard, but his eyes seemed watery. He didn't say a thing—just stared at them that way for a long time.

Solomon Parker had never realized that Mrs. Drummond had brought her identical sisters in to live with them. They'd practically had a palace all to themselves. Oh, they'd taken turns waiting on Mr. Parker, of course, but only as much as they had to.

Suddenly Mrs. Drummond broke down in tears. "I'm sorry, Solomon," she sniffled. "I was just afraid it would all be too much for you—getting back into the business."

"But you knew how much I wanted to run a railroad," Solomon said, clearing the lump in his throat at the same time. "All those years, I could have been living my dream."

"But then I would have lost you," she cried.

"You mean, you and your sisters would have lost your life of comfort."

The truth was they had gone to a lot of trouble to keep that life. To hide their little secret, they'd refused to hire live-in servants, which a house that large definitely needed. Instead they'd paid a small cleaning crew to take good care of their part of the house—the first floor. But to save money, the rest of the house—Mr. Parker's rooms—was left to gather dust and cobwebs.

"All those years ... what a fool I was to let you steal my life," the elderly man said, shaking his head. "Yes, it was as much my fault as yours, I suppose. I was so buried in self-pity that I surrendered everything of value to the taking."

"It ... it wasn't the money, really it wasn't," Mrs. Drummond argued, with a quick glance up toward his sister. "I ... I was afraid you wouldn't need me anymore."

"Everyone needs somebody, whether they know it or not," he answered.

Beamer and Scilla looked at Jack when they heard those words. They'd finally talked Jack into coming out of hiding for Mr. Parker's homecoming. Jack felt the heat of their gaze. He tried to laugh it off but ended up just lowering his head.

"Wait here," Solomon told the kids and shuffled off down the hallway.

Solomon's limousine driver walked in and began taking out the women's luggage. Another servant—Solomon's new butler—hurried down the hallway and took out more pieces. Ms. Parker barked orders down the second-story hallway, and three of Solomon's new maids came bustling down the staircase to help tote the last of the luggage.

Ms. Parker again fixed her hard eyes on the three women and said simply, "Leave now." Her heavy, velvety voice seemed to roll around the walls of the huge entry hall like a cannon ball.

Mrs. Drummond and her sisters flinched in fear and quickly scurried toward the door. The deposed assistant, the original Mrs. Drummond, was still wiping her eyes and sniffling pitifully. Scilla, however, thought she caught a piercing glance as Mrs. Drummond passed the kids. The butler scrambled back in, and the maids hurried upstairs to resume their cleaning. Moments later, Scilla heard the car engine rev up and then fade into the distance as it drove away with the three Drummond ladies.

Solomon Parker reappeared, carrying a notebook. "Come with me," he said as he walked by. "I have a little adventure for you." As they reached the door, he turned back and looked up toward his sister. He smiled and waved.

Scilla almost gasped as she saw the old woman's face crease into a tight smile. It wasn't the prettiest smile she'd ever seen. In fact, Scilla wouldn't have thought of it as a smile if she wasn't used to Ms. Parker's hard expression. For a moment, she was afraid the old lady's face might crack from the effort, but she didn't get to see because Solomon hustled Scilla out the front door before him.

Another limousine drove up as they walked out onto the porch. "I didn't know you had two limousines," Beamer said in amazement. This one was about twice the size of the other one and white instead of black.

"What kind of adventure are we going on?" Scilla asked as she turned back to Sol. "Are we goin' to your train set?"

"Maybe ... in a way," he said after a moment's pause. The driver opened double doors to let them enter the huge car. They plopped, laughing, into their long bench seat as the driver helped Sol get into the seat opposite them.

As they rode along, Sol spoke brightly of one project after another—the railroad he just found he owned and other projects for the city. First of all, though, he said he was going to open up his train set to visitors during the holidays. Secondly, he'd made a deal with the Middleton City Council to repair the trolley station and fix up the trolley cars. Yep, he was going to revive trolley service for tourists when they were visiting the more picturesque parts of downtown Middleton.

Beamer had never thought of Middleton as much of a tourist attraction. After all, Disneyland it was not. What was the big deal about a river and a bunch of old boats and buildings? Clearly they were something only adults, with their aged imaginations, could enjoy.

When the car finally reached its destination downtown, the kids scooted out to see a huge white wall with the name of a railroad etched deeply into its stone surface. Sol was taking them on a tour of his real, live railroad company—the one he had been growing stocks in all those years. Of course, he wasn't personally giving the tour. He left that to people who really knew where everything was. As the major stockholder, he was a kind of honorary boss and could get people to do that.

The railroad control center into which they were brought was like the bridge of Darth Vader's star destroyer. There were huge wall displays with the track systems, locomotives, cars, and other parts of a railroad operation mapped out in lights. Computers were placed around the interior like they were at NASA control. As far as Beamer was concerned, he couldn't have had more fun if he *was* at Disneyland. From the look on Ghoulie's face, Beamer suspected that he had a similar feeling. Scilla kept scooting from one end of the lighted wall chart to the other, seemingly fascinated by the system organization. More and more, that seemed to be Scilla's thing—organizing. Nowadays, everything on the tree ship had to have its place. Sooner or later, Beamer figured she was going to start trying to organize him. That would not be a good day.

Beamer looked around for Jack, wondering what was

going through his mind. Beamer finally saw him leaning against the water cooler with his hands in his pockets. He had a strange, wistful look as he gazed at all the electronic marvels. Beamer walked over next to him. "Well, whaddya think?" he asked the street kid.

With the colored lights from the wall display reflecting across his face, Jack said, "I'm thinkin' that anythin' like this is way beyond the reach of a kid livin' on the streets."

Beamer reached into his pocket and pulled out a piece of paper which he handed to Jack.

"What's this?" Jack asked.

"Your mother's address," he said as he watched the look on Jack's face. "It took a zillion phone calls, but my mom finally found it. Turns out your mom *had* to move when your dad died. She couldn't afford to keep up the house payments. My mom also found out that she's been through a drug-rehab program."

"You know," said Scilla as she suddenly appeared next to them, "in all your talk about not needin' your mom, have you ever thought that she might need you?"

"Yeah," added Beamer, "You just might have given up on your family a little too soon."

Later that evening, Beamer thought about the idea of "giving up." Giving up seemed to be a much bigger deal than Beamer had thought. Solomon Parker's dream had finally arrived — a little revised from his original one and much overdue. It was sad to think that if Solomon hadn't given up on God all those years ago, his revised dream might have come much sooner.

Beamer decided he was in no way about to give up on sports. He was going to make a few changes, though. Prompted by Jack's lessons in the trolley yard, Beamer would switch from baseball and begin playing in one of the football leagues the next fall. He wasn't all that big, but he hoped that he had enough coordination to duck his head and run with the ball. Actually, he figured he was pretty good on his feet, or he wouldn't have been able to do so much twisting, dodging, burrowing, and spinning to evade Jared and the other bullies that popped up from time to time.

Yep, dreams are kind of tricky, thought Beamer as he rummaged through the tree ship looking for wrapping paper. *Things happen — unexpected things, scary things — and it's easy to get discouraged.* But Beamer was just beginning to learn that, no matter what happened, you couldn't give up on God. After all, if God made us — each one — special for a reason, he had to have a plan for us, right?

Where is that paper? Beamer asked himself. Tonight was Christmas Eve, and he still had to wrap and deliver the presents for Ghoulie and Scilla as well as his new friends at church. Here it was, his favorite time of year, and he'd almost missed it! But then, as things turned out, he'd probably helped give Solomon Parker the best Christmas present he'd ever gotten. What could be better than getting your life back? Sol had also gotten his sister back. *Chances are they'll be sharing Christmas dinner together.*

Beamer was sure he had brought the wrapping paper out to the tree ship yesterday, along with the box of presents. He remembered going through the attic. *That's where I must have left it.*

As Beamer tightroped the branches to his roof, his thoughts returned to Sol — and Weenoh too. After all, the way his people had altered their dreams to create a whole new civilization was totally awesome. *Yep, no question about it — if you trusted, even in the darkest times, that the Lord*

wouldn't desert you, you just might find that God has laid out
another dream for you even bigger than the one you first imagined.
All you had to do was hang on for the ride.

Beamer scrambled up the roof and stepped through the
window. The afternoon sun filtered through the branches
of the tree and cast a dappled glow on the great web. For a
moment the web looked like a city as seen from an airplane,
with lights shimmering gold amid shadows of the night. It
took his breath away. Then he saw something else that really
sucked out his breath.

A cold chill sizzled down Beamer's back like frozen
lightning. The scientific equipment that had surrounded
the web all these months—that buzzing, blipping, beep-
ing, flashing electronic wonderland that had made their
attic look like something out of a sci-fi movie—was dead.
It was a strangely chilling sight—like seeing a room full of
mummies in an Egyptian tomb. They no longer looked like
machines, for each was cocooned in a thick coat of spider
silk, as if they had been flies caught in the web and painfully
deprived of their life juices.

Beamer stepped back out of the attic as his eyes scanned
the dark ceiling. There was only one explanation for all
this—Molgotha . . . was *back*!!

Scilla

Beamer

Ghoulie

Character Bios

Priscilla Bruzelski:
Age: 12 / 6th grade, Hair/Eyes: dishwater-blonde/green, Height: 4'9"

"*Scilla*" refuses to be called by her full name because it's too prissy for this tomboy. She is smaller than your average twelve-year-old, but she makes up for her small stature with a fiercely independent, feisty personality. She lives with her grandmother whom she was sent to live with when her single mother remarried. She has a half-brother named Dashiell who lives with her mother and her mother's new husband. Her grandmother takes her to church every Sunday out of tradition. Scilla loves climbing trees, football, basketball, and anything that's not girly. She doesn't get along with the popular girls at school, but she doesn't mind. She has strong opinions and will fight for what she believes is right.

Benson McIntyre:
Age: 13 / 7th grade, Hair/Eyes: short, wavy, sandy brown hair/blue, Height: 5'

"*Beamer*," named from the famous "Beam me up Scotty" line in *Star Trek*, has an interest in all things science fiction. He hates his given name, so don't call him Benson. You might get a response in wry, sarcastic humor from this energetic teenager. He recently moved with his family from Southern California to Middle America. He has a younger brother named Michael and an older sister named Erin. His father, referred to as "Mr. Mac," is a theater director, and his mother is a pediatrician called "Dr. Mac." He loves playing on the computer, likes keeping up with the times, and considers himself on the cutting edge. Coming from a strong Christian family, he analyzes all problems with deep spiritual thought. His love for science extends to his speech, as he often speaks in sci-fi space metaphors.

Garfunkel Ives:
Age: 12 / 7th grade, Hair/Eyes: black/brown, Height: 4'10"

"*Ghoulie*" got his name from the wide-eyed look he makes when he is excited. He's an intelligent boy who skipped a grade. He's small for his age and is the typical nerd who loves gadgets and computers, which makes him fodder for bullies. The constant bullying makes him jaded and sarcastic, and he would love to get revenge on the bullies. His father is a successful CFO of a large corporation and his mother is a highly-respected lawyer. His parents have little time for a spiritual life — or him — and have left his upbringing to the nanny. His parents have also left him with an extensive computer and gadget collection which he loves to use to quench his thirst for scientific knowledge.

The Star-Fighters of Murphy Street

Escape from the Drooling Octopod!

Robert West

kidz

1

Flight of the Pink Carpet

Beamer didn't have a clue where he was. He just woke up and ... *boing!*—he was circling in the air around a castle. He'd have preferred an F–18 or a stealth fighter. What did he get? A flying carpet. Talk about obsolete! He could forget Mach one. "Skateboard one" was probably pushing it. What was worse, the carpet had a temper. *How do you hang on to these things?* "Whoa!" he yelped as he was suddenly flipped into the air. He managed to grab hold of the carpet's fringe just as it dived through a large window in the castle. "Whaaaaoooooooooo," he exclaimed as his stomach turned inside out.

Incidentally, the castle was pink ... yeah, pink, as in bubble gum, peppermint sticks, and Barbie toys. Come to think of it, so was the carpet—pink, that is. He hated pink. That was the color his big sister, Erin, wore all the time. Frankly, if he wasn't dipping through the hallways of the castle and holding on for dear life, he'd never have taken a flying pink carpet seriously.

The next thing Beamer knew, he was on the floor looking up at a pink crystal chandelier about the size of his house. *Whoa! If that thing falls on me, I'll be a sparkly porcupine—not to mention dead.* It seemed like a good idea to get out from under it, but, for some reason, he couldn't move. He felt like he was wearing a straitjacket. He tried to wiggle free—no such luck. Then he looked down. That rascally carpet had wrapped around him like a cocoon. *Great! Now he was a bug in a rug!* "A little breathing room, please!" he called out to the carpet.

That was when Beamer noticed that he was rolled up at the foot of a huge pink staircase. It was shaped sort of like an hourglass, narrower in the middle than at the top or bottom. For all he knew, this could have been the very staircase where Cinderella lost her glass slipper. Why anyone would wear a glass slipper was beyond him. One step is all it would take for his sister to crunch it into smithereens. *Then she could forget being found by the prince who was posing as a would-be shoe salesman. Of course, if the only way this prince guy could recognize her was by her shoe size, he probably needed glasses as thick as binoculars. Either that or the fairy's spell on Cinderella included some major plastic surgery.*

Suddenly Beamer heard loud crunching and splintering. He jerked his head up to see an elephant swinging on the chandelier. Yep, you guessed it—a pink elephant! The big pachyderm was filling the air with pink glass like a hailstorm.

Then Beamer heard something groaning and then wailing in a high pitch. *The chandelier is about to fall!* Beamer twisted and turned, trying to get the carpet rolling. But instead of rolling across the room, he started rolling up the stairs! *Hey, what happened to gravity? You can't roll up stairs!* But then, what else could he expect from a flying carpet? "Ow! Ow! Hey! Whoa!" he yelped as he bumped along, lickety-split, up the stairs. The staircase must have been much taller than he thought. He just kept on bumping and rolling without coming to the top of the stairs. Of course, he wasn't seeing things all that well. Spinning around in that rug was making him pretty dizzy. Everything was swirling around like a pink tornado.

Beamer finally thudded to a stop. As the whirl of pink in his head slowed down, he noticed that he was no longer on the stairs. He also began having second thoughts about what he was wrapped up in. It wasn't a rug or a carpet or a straitjacket anymore. He was in a cocoon—a pink cocoon! What was worse, he was stuck in the middle of a huge pink spiderweb! He twisted and kicked, trying to break out of the cocoon. The web shook beneath him. Pretty soon it was shaking even more. He strained to tilt his head back. Then he saw it—a pink nightmare whose eight legs were churning in perfect order across the web. Soon he was going to be one big Slurpee for that hairy spider behemoth.

Soon it would be all over—no obituary, no tombstone, no nothing. Since none of this could possibly be real, Beamer MacIntyre wasn't even going to be history—he was just one more fantasy character crumpled and tossed in the trash can. He flailed about one last time, trying to escape—

Beamer thumped on a hard surface. "Ow!" he yelped in pain. Anxiously, he fought the confinement of the cocoon. Finally, he threw it off. But it wasn't a cocoon anymore. It was a blanket—his sister's pink quilt! *Yech! No wonder everything was pink.* His blanket must have been in the wash and his mom snuck his sister's on his bed under the bedspread. He looked up and saw the ceiling with the ice-cream-cone water stain. He was back in his bedroom, on the floor next to his bed. *It was all a dream—a silly old dream.* He sighed. *Talk about twisted fairy tales!*

"Beamer, you'll be late for school!" his mom called from the kitchen downstairs. "Stove, plate fo'ah low. Toastah own!" he heard her say. The only way to get the kitchen appliances to work in this house was to talk to them. But you had to talk to them nicely and in a Southern accent. Californian wouldn't cut it. That's where Beamer had come from—California. Living on Murphy Street in Middle America was turning out to be a whole new ball game.

"Mo-o-o-o-ommm!" a shrill voice shouted at the same time. "Where are my pink Nikes?" It was Beamer's big sister, Erin, otherwise known as Zero, Zero, Zero (0,0,0). Those are the coordinates for the center of the universe, which is what she thought she was. It was totally disgusting. As far as she was concerned, everyone and everything else in the universe revolved around her.

Also, at the same time, Beamer heard alternating thumping and slapping sounds on the staircase. That was the sound of a strange quadruped named Michael, his nine-year-old brother, who always came up the steps on all fours.

The last set of sounds came from his dad in the shower: "Too hot, too hot!" he said to the plumbing. "*Caolder, caolder, caolder* ... ahhhh, *jaust raight.*"

This was why Beamer didn't have many sleepovers at his house.

* * * * *

During history class, it finally occurred to Beamer where at least part of his dream had come from. It should have been obvious. *It was the web!—his web!* Nearly two stories tall and as wide as the house, the famous MacIntyre Web was the nightmare in the attic—the greatest entomological mystery this side of Cleveland.

Up until Christmas, the scientists experimenting on the web in their attic weren't even sure that it was a real web. Some thought it was man-made, somebody's joke or a hobby project or a mad scientist's experiment. But back on Christmas Eve, Molgotha, the web maker, had returned. She'd spun a cocoon around every piece of scientific equipment surrounding the web. Then she sucked the electronic life out of them, leaving them totally useless, as dead as the flies in the little web under the corner gutter.

So now, scientists from all over the country were in the MacIntyre attic, hovering around the web, hooking up this and that sensor. More than ever, the attic looked like the bridge of Darth Vader's Star Destroyer. Cameras now monitored the web 24–7, and multiple alarm systems registered every movement. The only reason the MacIntyres were still willing and able to live in the house was because the scientists calculated that all of the security systems gave the spider only "one chance in a hundred" of getting down where they lived. Of course, that "one chance in a hundred" was covered by family prayers every night. How many spiders do you know of that get into people's prayers?

That was three months ago. Spring vacation was only a half circle of the moon away, and still nobody knew who or why or what Molgotha was all about. Part of Beamer hoped they never would. It was kind of cool having a big mystery in your attic, except for the fact that it gave you the heebie-jeebies every time you got near it. You could never lose the feeling that Molgotha was up there somewhere, hiding in the shadows, smackin' her chops for your yummy red corpuscles.

We want to hear from you. Please send your comments about this
book to us in care of zreview@zondervan.com. Thank you.

ZONDERVAN.com/
AUTHORTRACKER
follow your favorite authors